Item:
shov
borro
telep
barc
This
Rene
Fines
incur
be ch

Lea

Baile
Dubli

Valley of Thunder

Josh Ford was the best man the Marshal Service had, so when the Governor of Montana needed someone to look into the disappearance of wagon trains in the Bitterroots, Ford was the man they chose.

What he found was a brutal autocrat who ruled with such terror, the like of which had never been seen by Ford.

From Helena, Montana, to the Bitterroot Mountains, then on to Seattle, Ford fights for his life and the lives of others against a maniac and his small army.

When a final twist puts it all in jeopardy, Ford realizes that the badge he wears may be the difference between law and justice.

Valley of Thunder

Sam Clancy

A Black Horse Western

ROBERT HALE

© Sam Clancy 2017
First published in Great Britain 2017

ISBN 978-0-7198-2157-8

The Crowood Press
The Stable Block
Crowood Lane
Ramsbury
Marlborough
Wiltshire SN8 2HR

www.bhwesterns.com

Robert Hale is an imprint
of The Crowood Press

This one is for Sam and Jacob.

Typeset by
Derek Doyle & Associates, Shaw Heath
Printed and bound in Great Britain by
CPI Group (UK) Ltd, Croydon, CR0 4YY

CHAPTER 1

Ten white canvas-covered wagons lumbered slowly along the trail, each drawn by teams of four oxen. Like giant beasts in a foreign land, the unwieldy conveyances lurched across the rough ground as they passed through a high country meadow filled with wildflowers.

Headed deeper into the Bitterroot mountains for a small valley called Parsons, were ten families intent on making their fortune on a new gold and silver strike. The valley was named for the man who'd made the initial discovery.

A scout and a wagon boss accompanied the group.

High above the wagon train, an eagle circled and looked down upon the serpent that weaved its way along the trail. To the south, on a low ridge dotted with larch and spruce, a large mountain lion sat atop one of many immense slabs of granite.

It patiently surveyed the strange beasts that travelled through its domain. It caught the scent of an elk on the slight breeze and with a low growl, abandoned its post and slunk off into the trees to hunt.

5

Another hunter, however, had his sights on the same beast. With a slow release of breath, Matt Smith squeezed the trigger of the Marlin lever-action rifle.

It bucked against his shoulder and the .45-70 round exploded from the octagonal barrel. It crossed the short distance between hunter and elk in the blink of an eye and hit the animal hard.

Smith watched as the animal buckled and went down. It kicked spasmodically then was still.

The wagon train scout stood up from his firing position behind the fallen tree and stretched out to his full six foot two height. He was thin and his buckskins hung loosely from his wiry frame. Before he moved, his brown eyes scanned their immediate surroundings but didn't detect anything unusual.

With the Marlin held across his body, Smith stepped over the rough-barked tree and moved to the fallen elk. Before he crouched down to butcher the carcase, he took another look about.

He had a bizarre sense of being watched. He scanned the ridge and the trees on it but saw nothing. With a shrug of his shoulders, Smith drew his knife, knelt down beside the dead animal and commenced work.

Orange flames licked hungrily at the elk haunch that hung over the fire. Droplets of fat sizzled and caused flares with each drip. The cooking flesh gave off a heavenly aroma and the smell permeated the still evening air.

Smith walked outside the wagon ring and stared off into the darkness. The silvery glow from the moon cast enough pale light across the landscape for the scout to make out the outline of the Bitterroot's high peaks that bordered the valley.

The lonesome howl of a wolf sounded closer than it was, carried on the chill night breeze.

A tingle ran down Smith's spine and he dropped his hand to the Colt at his hip. He wore it high, not low as gunfighters preferred, but he was a scout, not a gunman. A nervous scout, he was still unable to shake the uneasy feeling he'd felt this afternoon when he'd shot the elk.

Smith turned to his right and began to walk the perimeter of the circled wagons. He checked the night pickets and as he walked, long, damp grass gently caressed his legs.

The muffled snort of a horse caused Smith to pause. He peered into the gloom and saw the animal twenty yards from the encampment.

He watched for a moment, suspicious of the cause, but relaxed a little when it continued to graze.

Smith shook his head and silently cursed its owner for not securing it better. As he approached, the animal lifted its head and looked in Smith's direction.

It tossed its head and stepped closer to a clump of shrubs and once again began to crop grass.

The scout spoke in soft tones to the horse and closed the gap between them as he aimed to get close enough to grab its halter rope.

He heard the wolf again and the horse tossed its head around once more. Smith continued to speak gently and kept his approach smooth and steady.

When he got close, he reached out carefully to take hold of the rope.

Smith sensed a movement behind him. He dropped his hand to the Colt and began to turn.

Before he could draw, a thorny hand clamped firmly over his mouth, which prevented the escape of any sound from his throat.

The next sensation he experienced was a searing pain as a knife slid between his ribs and pierced his heart.

'Damn it, where is that man?' wagon master Earl Morgan blustered as he roamed the bevy of activity as camp broke.

He'd made three circuits but still couldn't find the scout, Smith.

He was about to ask one of the settlers when he heard a cry of, 'Riders approaching'.

Morgan spun his six foot frame around to gaze in the direction of the riders. The 41-year-old frowned, and wondered who had ridden up to them. His first thought was Smith so he hurried to a better vantage point. Morgan's hope died when he saw two riders and realized that neither was the missing scout.

His weathered face fell further when he saw a body draped over a horse.

The wagon master moved to meet them and was joined by two others. Both were family men who'd uprooted their wives and children to drag them halfway across the country at the prospect of a rich strike. Their names were Otis and Cohen.

The strangers drew up in front of the three men.

'Howdy, gents,' greeted a man in trail-stained buck-skins. 'You wouldn't be missin' someone by any chance?'

Morgan eyed the strangers cautiously. He guessed the man in the buckskins to be mid-thirties. His face was lined and had a scar on one cheek. His partner was late twenties, slim built and wore britches and a faded red shirt under a buckskin coat. Both men rode bay horses.

'Maybe,' Morgan said. 'Who are you?'

'I'm Roy,' the man answered. 'This is Hitch.'

'We found this here feller out aways. Looks like Indians have been at him. Took his scalp, they did.' Roy pointed to the body on the chestnut horse they'd lead in.

Morgan moved closer and tentatively lifted the dead man's head. His stomach churned when he saw that it was indeed their scout and the ghastly deeds which had been done to him. Apart from being scalped, his eyes were gone and there was an ugly slash across his face.

Morgan let the head down and turned away from the grisly sight.

'Who is it?' Otis asked.

'It's Smith,' Morgan said, his voice tinged with sadness.

'Damn it,' Cohen cursed softly.

'Yep,' Hitch cackled. 'Damn Nez Perce sure did make a mess of him. Peeled his hair off, as neat as you like.'

Hitch!' Roy snapped. 'Show a little respect. These here gents have just lost a friend of theirs.' The young stranger smiled but remained silent.

Morgan shook his head. 'This is the first we've seen of Indians.'

'The Nez Perce have been actin' up a bit around here lately,' Roy explained. 'With all the whites comin' into the territory, they were bound to get upset.'

'What are we goin' to do without a guide?' said Otis, concern evident in his voice.

'Well now, if it's a guide you all need, we can do that for you,' Roy offered. 'We know the country around here like the backs of our hands. Where you all headin' anyways?'

'We're headin' to Parsons,' Morgan said.

Roy smiled. 'Hell, we know that place. Are you all out to strike it rich?'

'Hopefully.' Otis nodded.

'We know a way that'll get you there a week shy of when you was expectin' to get there yourselves.' Roy smiled. 'If you want the help, we'll guide you. The cut-off will keep you clear of the Nez Perce, too.'

Morgan shifted uneasily. 'I ain't so sure. . . .'

'I think we should do it,' Cohen said eagerly.

Morgan hit him with a hard stare. 'Who's bossin' this here train?'

'Don't you think we should take 'em up on their offer?' Otis said. 'We need a guide to get us there. And if they can save us a week of travellin' time, it'll be worth it.'

Morgan knew he was right. He looked up at Roy. 'How much do you want for guidin' us?'

'Fifty dollars, each,' Roy said. 'I'll do the guidin' and Hitch here will keep us in fresh meat.'

The wagon master thought for a moment then asked, 'Where is this cut-off you was talkin' about?'

'You follow the trail for half a day then you come to a ridge line with an opening on the right,' Roy said. 'It looks to be all choked up with some big old fir trees. But

10

the trail cuts right on through and opens out the other side. Indians don't go in there because they think it's haunted or somethin'.'

Satisfied, Morgan nodded. 'All right then, you've got yourselves a job. You'll be paid once we get to the diggin's.'

'Right you are,' said Roy in acceptance of the terms. 'Let's get these wagons rollin'.'

Twenty minutes later, the wagon train was back on the trail. Smith had been buried in an unmarked grave off to the side. Within a year, no sign would remain, and the probability was that his existence would not be remembered. Not long after noon, the wagon train reached the tree-choked pass. It turned right and disappeared amongst tall, rough-barked firs.

Unseen by the travellers were two Nez Perce warriors seated upon fine dappled mounts. They observed from the shelter of a large stand of trees, obscured by the shadows the giants cast.

They'd seen wagons enter the valley beyond many times before, but none had ever re-emerged.

The Nez Perce had a name for it. They called it the 'Valley of Thunder'.

CHAPTER 2

Every step promised the wet slop and squelch of mud. An afternoon storm had dumped sheets of rain upon the town of Spencer's Gulch, Montana. It had ceased an hour before but the far off rumble of thunder was still audible. Overhead, leaden clouds blocked the sun and cast a gloom over the main street.

Townsfolk lined the plank boardwalks to watch the spectacle. One man against three. Near impossible odds but they stood with baited breath in the hope that the one would carry the day.

Josh Ford let his hand drop to the walnut grips of the single-action Colt Peacemaker nestled in a black leather holster.

He kept up a steady pace and the citizens watched the passive face of the man in black.

Up ahead, Ford's steely gaze settled on the three men who blocked his path. Their names were Buford Welsh, Dwight Williams, and Jesse O'Rorke.

Sheriff Buford Welsh was forty-one and mean. He was tall and wore a full suit, similar to a dandy. About his hips was a gun belt which housed a new Smith & Wesson model.

Deputies Dwight Williams and Jesse O'Rorke were dressed in jeans, shirt and a leather vest. Both men had Remington six-guns in their holsters. The ambidextrous O'Rorke favoured two.

The town of Spencer's Gulch had experienced a reign of tyranny and fear from the three since last fall. The previous long-standing sheriff had fallen to their guns and they'd taken his badge.

After months of brutality against the townsfolk, the men were about to learn the error of their ways.

The distant rumble of thunder rolled across the heavily wooded mountains, a death knell for those about to die.

Ford squelched to a stop twenty feet from the men. Close enough for them to see the nickel plated marshal's badge pinned to his chest.

'Time for you three to throw down them guns of yours and take off them badges you're tarnishing,' Ford said evenly.

'Do you really expect us to do that, Ford?' Welsh sneered.

'It's either that or they'll be carryin' you off the street feet first.'

Welsh smiled coldly. 'Big talk for a man who's facin' three guns. What chance do you think you've got?'

'You know, you may be right,' Ford allowed. 'Just to get things straight. Do you intend to disarm?'

'No,' Welsh confirmed. 'Can't kill you if we do that.'

Ford nodded. 'OK.'

His hand blurred as it brought up the Peacemaker. Flame spewed from the gun barrel as he fanned the hammer. The thunder of the shots rang out across the main street of Spencer's Gulch.

The move was unexpected and Welsh didn't even register surprise on his face before the first bullet tore through his chest. The second one hit him in the throat and as it exited, took a fine spray of warm blood.

Ford shifted his aim and the slug he fired at O'Rorke smashed into the outlaw's forehead. A third eye appeared and stopped his draw cold. The six-gun, half drawn from its holster, dropped back as nerveless fingers lost their grip.

As Ford's Peacemaker settled on Williams, the hammer on the outlaw's Remington fell. The .44 calibre slug burned through the air and fanned Ford's cheek.

The marshal fired again, his shot more accurate than the outlaw's, and the bullet punched into Williams's chest high and left. The impact spun him around and sent him to his knees. The wound made Williams cry out with pain.

Ford eared back the hammer on the Peacemaker. The triple-click of its action was reminiscent of the snap of a dry twig.

Williams struggled around to bring his Remington to bear.

'Don't!' Ford snapped as the wounded outlaw started to raise his gun.

'Go to hell!' Williams snarled, his voice thick with pain and hate.

'I'll have to meet you there,' Ford told him and

squeezed the trigger.

Once again, the Colt roared and Williams flopped back into the mud, dead.

Ford let the Colt drop to his side. Small wisps of grey-blue gun smoke drifted from the barrel. He studied the downed men. He looked for signs of life but all remained still. Satisfied, Ford reloaded his six-gun with fresh rounds.

As he stood in the mud of the main street, the eyes that beheld him would have had him distinctly pegged as much taller than his six foot one. He was solidly built and dressed in black, and resembled a mortician more than a United States Marshal.

The relief exuded by the onlookers on the crowded boardwalks was palpable.

Ford glanced one last time at the bodies and turned away. He began his walk back along the street when a horse and rider caught his attention.

An older man with greying hair and a salt and pepper moustache and lined face sat ramrod erect in his saddle. He rode a large buckskin gelding with a high step.

When he drew the horse to a halt in front of Ford, he glared at the marshal.

'Damn it, Ford!' he cussed. 'You were told to damn well wait.'

An hour later, both men sat in the Jack of Spades saloon at a dark timber table with a polished but scarred top. The place was abuzz with excitement after the events witnessed that very day.

Cigarette smoke hung thick in the air. Glasses clinked

together and raised voices grew louder as every man in the saloon related their own personal version of what they'd seen.

Outside, the daylight was almost gone, while inside, lamps mounted on wood-panelled walls cast a dull light around the bar room.

Out of the crowd, a loud rebel yell echoed throughout the saloon.

United States Marshal Bass Reeves screwed his face up in contempt. 'Anyone would think you were a blamed hero the way they're carryin' on. Instead, you disobeyed orders to wait for help to arrive. I'm startin' to get fed up with this lone wolf attitude of yours, Josh.'

Josh Ford had heard it all before and was only half tuned into his boss's berating.

'. . . and then it'll be too late and you'll already be dead.'

Reeves paused, then, 'Are you listening to me?'

'Nope,' Ford said truthfully.

Reeves snorted. 'You'll never learn, will you?'

'I work alone, Bass. You know that.'

'Yeah, but it may very well get you killed one day, too.'

'When it does, don't bother comin' to my funeral,' said Ford. 'The last thing I need to hear when they're plantin' me is you sayin' "I told you so".'

'Damn stubborn boy,' Reeves said. 'Just like your old man.'

'Yeah, well, the apple doesn't fall far from the tree, does it, Bass?'

'And maybe one day you'll call me Pa instead of by my first name,' Reeves said and tossed back a shot of red-eye.

16

'Not likely.'

Ford's father had left when Josh was still a young boy. He'd gone to fight in the War Between the States and never come home. Over the years, there had been letters to his mother, which he hadn't known about until after her death.

It was from this correspondence he'd gleaned that his father was a United States Marshal. Years of anger and frustration were pent up and he set out to get answers from the man who'd abandoned them long ago.

Instead of shooting Bass Reeves, Ford had joined the Marshals. At which time, his father became his boss.

Reeves had been wary of the hot-headed young man at first, but now, ten years on, Josh was a top line deputy who'd brought more killers to heel than anyone cared to count.

'What are you doin' here, Bass?' Ford asked his father. 'You could have sent any number of marshals to help out. Instead, you come to Spencer's Gulch yourself.'

Reeves's face took on a grave expression. 'The governor wants to see you, boy. There's been some strange goin's on in the Bitterroots and he wants the best man we have to go and check it out.'

'What strange goin's on?'

Reeves shook his head. 'I don't know the whole story. Apparently wagon trains have been disappearin' and he wants us to check it out. When you leave here, you're to go to see him. He'll fill you in.'

Ford drank what was left of his beer and placed the mug on the table.

'Fair enough. I'll leave first thing in the mornin'.'

Reeves's grave expression never changed.

'You be careful out there, Josh,' Reeves warned. 'It would be an inconvenience if you were to go and get yourself killed. If you need help, you know where to find us.'

CHAPTER 3

In 1864, it was a mining camp called Last Chance Gulch. Now Helena was a bustling, sprawling city of 5,000 citizens and growing fast.

When Ford rode into Helena on a big, mean tempered blue roan, it was late in the afternoon and the sun had started to drop behind the distant mountains.

He found a livery stable for the horse which cost four bits a day plus feed. Ford warned the hostler to watch himself around the spiteful animal.

'He'll bite, kick, butt with his head or try to stomp you if you're not careful,' Ford had said.

To which the hostler replied, 'Then why not shoot him and be done with it?'

'Because he's the best damned horse I ever had,' Ford answered and left the man who stood and scratched his head incredulously.

As he trudged along the dusty main street, he carried his Winchester rifle and saddle-bags. Ford came across a hotel dubbed quite simply the Helena Hotel.

The marshal stomped up onto the boardwalk, eased

past a pair of men who stood talking just outside the doorway, and pushed his way into the hotel lobby.

From the outside, the hotel appeared to be an upstanding establishment and once inside, he could see that his assumption had been correct.

The floor of the foyer was covered in brown carpet while the patterned paper on the walls, wall lamps, and polished counter gave it a touch of class. The stairs had hand-tooled balustrades and the top of the landing was wide and gave access to hallways which ran in both directions.

As Ford walked over to the counter, a well-dressed gentleman in a suit, string tie, polished shoes and smoking a cigar came down the stairs. He looked Ford over with a hint of indignation on his face.

'Howdy,' Ford greeted him.

The man ignored him and walked past him as if he weren't there and kept going.

'Nice to meet you, too,' Ford called after him. Then added, 'Stuck up jackass.'

'Ahem?'

Ford turned to find a middle-aged man, dressed in a suit, standing behind the counter with a stern look on his face.

'What's your problem?' Ford asked him.

'I'm sorry, sir, but we don't speak thus to the clientele.'

Ford stared at him for a moment then deliberately dumped his saddle-bags onto the counter top, followed by his rifle.

'Well, mister, how about giving me one of your rooms

so I can become one of those clientele fellers you're talkin' about.'

Disdain crept into the concierge's face as he looked the man who stood before him in trail-stained clothes, up and down. 'I'm sure a man such as yourself will be quite comfortable along the street at the Last Chance saloon. I'm positive it will suit your needs just fine.'

Ford became irritable and impatient with this officious desk clerk.

'Listen, sport,' he snapped as he placed his hand on the Winchester, 'I don't want to go to the saloon. I want a bed here. And a bath with hot water. So turn around and walk on over to that keyboard on the wall and get me a room key.'

The man stood there open mouthed. He'd never been spoken to in that manner before. And certainly not by trail trash.

'What are you waiting for?' Ford said. He grabbed the desktop ledger and continued. 'I'm going to sign this here book and if I don't have a key by the time I'm finished, I'm goin' to take up my Winchester and shoot you.'

'How dare you threaten me, sir,' the clerk said indignantly. 'I shall have to inform the local law about your behaviour.'

Ford drew back the left side of his jacket so the man could see the marshal's badge.

'How about you inform me,' he said. 'Then I shall inform the governor when I see him tomorrow that you had some troubles.'

The clerk opened his mouth to speak but snapped it

shut like a bear trap. He turned away to fetch a key.

'I thought so,' Ford mumbled.

The clerk dropped the key on the counter. 'Room eight, sir. It will be three dollars a night. In advance.'

'What about the bath?'

'All included, sir.'

Ford paid the man and lifted his gear from the counter.

'You'll find your room down the hallway to the right.'

Ford nodded and climbed the stairs. Right now he wanted a bath, a meal, and a good night's sleep.

'I said, you owe me a drink, stranger.' The man's aggressive stance sounded a warning bell in Ford's head. Then he dropped his right hand to the polished walnut grip of his Colt. 'Now how about you buy it for me before I take it out of your hide.'

'I'll tell you this one time, friend,' Ford cautioned in a low, menacing voice. 'If you don't take your hand away from that six-gun, I'll kill you where you stand.'

The crowd of onlookers shuffled back across the sawdust covered floor nervously.

Ford had come to the Last Chance saloon after his bath for a hot meal and a drink to wash the trail dust from his parched throat.

The meal consisted of steak, potatoes, and gravy. He followed it up with a dessert of apple pie and dumplings.

Once finished, Ford decided that he would buy a beer, drink it, then head back to the hotel.

As he approached the long hardwood counter, a percentage girl with long black hair moved towards him.

She wore a red dress that barely contained her ample breasts, and ran a long-fingered hand over his chest and shoulder. She winked at him.

'Care to buy me a drink, handsome?' she asked in her best seductive voice.

Ford removed her hand gently and shook his head. 'You're wastin' your time, ma'am.'

She pouted and walked gracefully off into the crowd.

It was then that Ford bumped into the man and spilled his beer.

'Let me tell you somethin', stranger,' he snarled. 'Matt Gibson don't scare too easy.'

Gibson was in his early thirties and had small beady eyes. His thin wiry frame stretched five ten from the floor and his face was a mix of lines and scars. Truly a man of the frontier, thought Ford. But what kind? Outlaw or . . .

'Well? I'm waiting,' Gibson sneered.

'Don't push me, Gibson,' Ford advised him. 'I only wanted a drink, not trouble.'

'Well, it's trouble you got. In spades.'

'Gibson, wait!' A voice cut through the tension.

Gibson turned his gaze toward the speaker. 'What do you want, Graf?'

'You'd best listen to him, Gibson, and haul back on your reins a might.'

'Why?'

'Don't you know who he is?' Graf asked with a hint of veiled excitement.

'No, damn it,' Gibson answered impatiently.

'That's Josh Ford,' Graf informed him in a hushed

tone, as though afraid Ford might overhear him. 'The US Marshal.'

Gibson's hand jumped away from the gun butt of his Colt as if it had turned scalding hot. A hint of uncertainty filtered into his eyes. 'Is that true?' Gibson asked.

Ford nodded. 'Yeah. Now get out of the saloon before you use up your last chance.'

Gibson opened his mouth to say something then thought better of it. Instead, he turned on his heel and headed for the door.

Strangely enough, Ford thought that it would not be his last encounter with Matt Gibson.

Governor Edmond Reynolds's thoughts were interrupted by the soft knock on the large mahogany door of his office. It swung open and a middle-aged woman entered.

'What is it, Meredith?' he asked in a deep voice.

'United States Marshal Josh Ford is here to see you, sir,' the woman announced.

Reynolds nodded. 'Send him in, please. Oh, and find Jeff Brady for me and have him come see me straight away.'

'Yes, sir.'

Meredith disappeared and moments later, Ford entered the room.

Reynolds climbed out of his leather, hand-carved chair and eased his large, suit covered frame around his desk.

He stuck out a meaty hand and said, 'Marshal Ford, I'm glad you could come so promptly.'

Ford took the hand in a firm grip and as he shook, he looked into grey eyes and tried to read the man.

Reynolds had turned sixty the previous month but his eyes still shone brightly with life.

'I wasn't given much choice, Governor. Marshal Reeves said it was urgent.'

The man's face turned grim. 'Indeed, it is, Marshal. Indeed, it is.'

'Call me Ford, Governor, or Josh. It makes no difference to me.'

Reynolds smiled. 'Fine, Ford it is.' He pointed to a chair. 'Take a seat. I'm just waiting for another man and we'll begin.'

Reynolds sat down again and Ford took the chance to look around the lavish office. It appeared, from the bearskin rug and the moose and deer heads, that the governor was a hunter of sorts.

However, he also had a decorated Blackfoot peace pipe on his desk. The windows were mullioned and all of the furniture was hand-carved from fine quality timber. What captured his eye the most was the portrait behind him. It depicted a colonel in the uniform of the Union cavalry. That man was Reynolds.

The governor noticed him looking at it.

'The old days, I'm afraid, Ford,' he explained. 'The portrait was done soon after the end of the War. I served with your father in fact.'

Ford nodded. 'That would explain why Bass himself rode to see me about the job instead of sending another man.'

'He's a good man, your father.'

25

'I'm afraid we'll have to disagree on that one, Governor.'

Reynolds nodded. Though he said nothing, the look on his face told Ford he knew of the differences between father and son.

Another knock on the door stopped further discussion on the topic, and when Ford turned, a man had entered the room.

He was around thirty years old and tall like Ford. His brown hair was combed neatly but his face was tanned. A sure sign that the man spent much of his time outdoors, although the suit he wore wouldn't be the most appropriate attire in the wilds.

'Come in, Jeff,' Reynolds invited the man. 'I want you to meet Josh Ford. He's the US Marshal I was telling you about.'

Ford looked at the governor who stared back at him, a hint of a smile on his face.

So the governor had asked for him personally.

'That's right, Ford, I asked for you.' It was as though he'd read Ford's mind. 'I've heard about your work and when I contacted your father, he told me that he'd send you. Before you say anything, it's all done now. You're here and that is the most important part. Now, meet Jeff Brady. He works for me personally and he'll work with you on this assignment.'

'Now hang on—'

'Pleased to meet you, Ford,' Brady interrupted and stuck out his hand.

Ford just looked at the proffered hand then turned his attention back to Reynolds.

'If you want my help, Governor, let's get one thing straight. I work alone.'

'Bass said those same words,' Reynolds elaborated. 'But on this job, you will work with Brady.'

Ford stood up and put his hat on his head. 'Sorry, Governor, tell Bass to find you another man.'

'That was the other thing Bass said. You are stubborn. He also said that's what makes you a good deputy marshal because you don't know when to give up.'

'Bass seems to have flapped his gums a lot about me.'

'At least do me the courtesy of hearing me out,' Reynolds urged him. 'And after I'm done, if you still want out, then you can go on your way and I'll tell Bass to find me someone else.'

Ford looked at him and fully intended to walk out without a backward glance. Instead, he sat back down.

'Thank you,' Reynolds said. 'Now, let's get started.'

CHAPTER 4

'So mostly this briefing, for want of a better word, is for you, Ford,' Reynolds explained. 'Brady already knows what I'm about to tell you.'

Ford said nothing when Reynolds paused.

'Right, I'll continue. I take it that you've heard of the Parson's strike in the Bitterroots?'

Ford nodded. 'I have.'

'Well, over the last eight months, numerous wagon trains have left here bound for that particular strike. However,' he paused for dramatic effect, 'five of those wagon trains have failed to reach their destination.'

'Nez Perce or outlaws?' asked Ford.

Reynolds shook his head. 'We don't know. They have just vanished. Around 110 men, women and children. There has been no sign of them whatsoever.'

Ford was surprised by this information. 'Surely someone must know something.'

'If they do, they aren't talking,' Brady said.

'Did you send a man out there to look around?'

'When it was brought to my attention three weeks

ago, I sent a man into the Bitterroots to look around,' Reynolds said.

'He disappeared, too,' Brady told Ford.

'So what is it you plan to do?' Ford said.

'The day after tomorrow, another wagon train is due to leave Helena,' Reynolds said. 'Jeff is going to scout for it.'

'So where do I come in?'

'I need you to shadow the wagon train and keep an eye on everythin',' Brady told him. 'I need someone I can count on to watch my back. And by all accounts, you're it.'

'Well, Ford, what's it going to be?' It was more a challenge than a question. 'Are you in or not?'

Ford already knew what the answer was going to be. 'All right, Governor, I'm in.'

Reynolds smiled. 'Good. I knew I could count on you.'

'Don't go getting ahead of yourself, Governor,' Ford cautioned him. 'Whatever or whoever is out there that can make over a hundred people disappear may be more than any one of us has bargained for.'

Morgan stumbled, fell, rose back up and kept running. A branch whipped across his face, opened his cheek with a deep cut that caused the blood to run freely.

He could hear them behind him, the gap closing all the time. His hunters were relentless.

Once again he fell, his right shoulder smashed into the trunk of an aspen and fingers of pain shot down his arm. He staggered to his feet and leaned against the tree.

He could hear them crash through the brush behind him and he lunged forward into another stumbling run.

His lungs burned for air and his leg muscles screamed for him to stop. To do so, though, would condemn him to death. His only chance of survival was to keep going.

Morgan burst from the large stand of aspen and out into the open. He stopped. He stood at the edge of a large meadow which was barely visible in the early grey-ness of the pre-dawn.

He immediately ruled out exposure in the open. Frantically he looked left and right. Right took him towards a wall of granite. A sheer rock face that looked impassable even in this light. His only alternative was left.

Morgan stayed in the tree-line and started to the left. His run was barely more than a shuffle. He'd run most of the night and it had taken its toll.

The noises behind him grew louder and Morgan looked back to check the proximity of his pursuers.

His foot caught on a fallen branch in the grass and he crashed heavily to the ground. His face buried in the wet grass, the smell strong, mixed with the odour of damp earth.

He lay there a moment and willed himself to use the last of his waning strength to push himself back to his feet.

Morgan rose to his knees and knew there would be no going on. He looked up at the trees and noticed that their tops were lit up as the sun crested the surrounding mountains. He thought it was a wondrous sight, fitting for it to be his last.

There came a crash through the brush and without turning to face his attacker, Morgan closed his eyes. Almost immediately, a snarling beast exploded from the trees and launched itself at Morgan.

The serenity of the forest was shattered and filled with the terrified dying screams of the wagon master and the snarls of his killer.

The old grey lobo slunk off down the back side of the ridge at the first approach of the rider. The strike of hoof on stone was enough to alert it to the intruder's presence.

Ford drew rein on the big blue roan just below the crest of the ridge and dismounted. He tied it to a low branch on a lodgepole pine then did the same to his pack horse on a different tree away from the roan. He edged his way over the top and sat on a flat rock beside a tall spruce.

Down below, he watched the wagon train snake along the valley floor. Nine wagons in all lumbered along the trail drawn by sturdy oxen.

From his vantage point, Ford could see both directions along the narrow, steep-sided valley and across to the far ridge line on the other side.

Both ridges were thickly wooded with fir, spruce, lodgepole pines and some aspen. Amongst them sat slabs of grey-faced rock, millions of years old like the valley.

Ford scanned the far ridge and could see nothing other than a large bull elk. The beast had the massive antler rack of an older male.

31

Ford sighed. The wagon train had been on the trail for two weeks and was now deep in the Bitterroots. In all that time, he'd seen nothing. He doubted whether anything would happen on this trip at all.

His attention was drawn back to the elk. It had moved and was faced back along the ridge where it stood. It remained still for what seemed to be an eternity before it broke into a sudden run and disappeared over the far side of the ridge line.

Ford frowned and steadily moved his gaze along the slope. Though he could see nothing, he was certain that the elk had seen or heard something to disturb it.

He watched patiently but still nothing moved. He didn't like it. A cold chill washed down his back. There was something out there and he knew that sooner or later, he would find out what.

Ford stood up and walked back over the ridge to where his horses waited.

'Good, he's gone,' said the first man with a hint of relief.

The second man nodded. 'I was beginnin' to think he'd seen us.'

Their names were Pike and Cross. Both men were wanted by the law in various parts of the west. They had killed before without compunction and would do so again.

'What are we goin' to do about him?' asked the tall, thin Cross. 'He's obviously shadowin' the train. That's the second time we've seen him.'

Pike nodded in agreement. 'Tonight we'll deal with him. We'll stay here until the wagon train is out of sight and slip across the valley. Once it gets dark, we'll close in and get rid of him.'

'Who do you reckon he is? Do you reckon he's from the same place as that other feller who came snoopin' around?' Cross meant the first man the governor had sent into the Bitterroots. The man they'd buried amongst a stand of aspen in an unmarked grave.

Pike was a solid built man in his early thirties. He took off his broad-brimmed hat and ran a calloused hand through his straw-like brown hair. 'It's possible,' Pike allowed. 'Maybe more than possible. Maybe the governor done sent out another feller to keep an eye on this train and find his missin' man.'

Without saying so, Pike thought that was exactly what had happened. He knew it was only a matter of time before someone started to seriously investigate the missing wagon trains.

It came as no surprise to him when the first man showed up looking around. Now Pike was beginning to think that maybe it was time to cut out before it all came crashing down around his ears. What would be next? The Army?

He decided that this would be his last train. After they were finished, he would leave quietly in the night and not return.

'Did you hear me?' Cross interrupted his thoughts.
'What?'
'I said the boss ain't goin' to like this.'
'No, he ain't.'

The small campfire crackled and popped as the orange-blue flames licked greedily at the dry sticks that Ford fed it.

Out in the darkness-clad wilderness, a wolf howled its low mournful sound. A great horned owl called from high up in a tall Douglas fir and was answered by another farther back in the forest.

Ford had found a place to camp behind the ridge and set up beside a small clear-water stream, which ran along the forested edge of the ridge's slope.

He decided that the following morning he would cross behind the wagon train to the other side of the valley to see if he could find any sign of whatever had startled the elk.

He sat hunched over a steaming cup of bitter black coffee. Between each sip, he blew gently on it to cool it a little.

Ford enjoyed the solitude that accompanied working alone. Though he was partnered with Brady this time, his vigil over the wagon train was still a solitary affair.

The cessation of forest noise which had filled the still night was the first indication that he was no longer alone. One moment the air was filled with a myriad of sounds, the next, an eerie silence.

The owl, high up in the fir tree, took sudden flight in a flurry of frantic flapping wings. Then the roan snorted and stomped a hoof.

The cup, held in Ford's left hand, paused on its way to his mouth. His right hand edged towards his Colt as his eyes searched the dark. There was no moon so the darkness was almost complete beyond the light of the small campfire.

The sound of a gun hammer going back spurred Ford into action. He lunged backward, threw the cup to one

34

side and drew the six-gun from its holster.

Thunder filled the night as rifle fire exploded from the trees at the edge of the camp. Orange tongues of flame lanced out as deadly lead tunnelled through the empty space where Ford had just been.

The marshal landed heavily and the hard ground jarred his whole body. Another flurry of shots rang out and Ford composed himself enough to fire back.

His Peacemaker barked and lead scythed into the darkness where the shots had come from.

A loud cry of pain was followed by the sound of a thud as a body fell heavily to the ground. A muffled curse told Ford that there was still at least one more assailant to worry about.

More rifle fire sounded and the bullets furrowed into the earth around Ford's feet. He rolled to the left and came up onto his knee, and fired two more shots.

Without warning, a man charged out of the darkness and into the firelight. His face was a mask of rage. He threw down his rifle and drew his six-gun.

'Damn you!' he shouted.

Ford took deliberate aim at the man and squeezed the trigger of his Colt. The gun bucked against his palm and the slug took the man dead centre.

The attacker stiffened and fell forward. He lay still, seemingly asleep in the campfire's glow.

Still on edge, Ford braced for more gunfire to erupt from the surrounding darkness but all remained silent.

He ejected the spent cartridges from his gun and reloaded then holstered it. He moved towards the dead man.

'Let's have a look at you,' he muttered.

Ten minutes later, Ford had the two dead men laid out beside the fire where there was enough light for him to see their faces. He knew them. Ford had seen the mugs of Pike and Cross before on wanted dodgers.

He couldn't be certain that they were tied up with what was happening in the Bitterroots.

That they had startled the elk earlier in the day was without question. He was also sure that they had seen him shadowing the wagon train.

He thought about the possibility of their involvement in the bigger picture.

If so, they may not be out here alone.

Ford made the decision that the following morning he would ride down to the wagon train and take the bodies with him.

CHAPTER 5

Brady saw Ford first. The wagons were set to move out when he noticed the rider approach with three horses in tow. Once closer, he recognized who it was.

'What the hell?' Brady cursed softly.

He spurred his horse forward and rode out to meet him. He drew up and stared at the bodies. His eyes narrowed and he turned his annoyed gaze on Ford.

'What the hell are you doin' here?' he hissed in a harsh whisper. 'You were told to remain out of sight. And who are the two fellers?'

Ford ignored Brady's open hostility.

'Their names are Pike and Cross,' he explained. 'There's paper on both of them. They decided to jump me last night on the other side of the ridge. What you should be askin' is why they were shadowin' the wagon train.'

Brady raised his eyebrows. 'Were they?'

Ford nodded. 'Almost certain of it.'

'You didn't happen to get a chance to ask 'em why?'

'Nope.'

There was a shout from the train and Ford and Brady looked in that direction. Two men approached on foot.

'Hell, that's all we need.' Brady sighed in frustration.

'You might want to consider this, too,' Ford said quietly. 'That feller on the left. His name is Gibson, right?'

'Yeah.'

'He knows me,' Ford said. 'Had me a run in with him in Helena. He knows I'm a marshal.'

'It just gets better, don't it.' Brady's voice dripped with sarcasm.

'Who's the other feller?' Ford asked.

'His name is Hayes,' Brady explained. 'He's the wagon master. Him and Gibson are friends.'

Ford frowned. 'How do they strike you?'

'Hayes seems to know what he's doin',' Brady said. 'Gibson, on the other hand, is trouble waitin' to happen. A couple of times he's had a run-in with a family man named Ellis. Has himself a daughter almost full growed. Gibson has taken a shine to her. One sided.'

Ford nodded. 'Somethin' tells me he's bad all the way through.'

'Yeah. You could be right.'

'What's goin' on here, Brady?' Hayes snapped as he stopped close to the two men. 'Who's this feller?'

The wagon master's weathered face grew lines as he frowned and looked at the two bodies draped over the horses.

'His name is—' Brady started.

'Is Ford,' Gibson cut in. 'He's a US Marshal.'

Hayes's grey eyes narrowed. 'Is that so?'

38

Ford nodded. After all, there was no use denying it.

Hayes was a tall man, with a large barrel chest. Ford figured him to be aged around thirty-eight.

'What brings you way out here, Marshal?' Hayes asked snidely.

'The governor was worried about a number of wagon trains that have gone missing of late,' Ford said truthfully. 'So I was asked to take a look. These two jumped me last night.'

Ford paused as Gibson moved around behind him to look at the bodies.

He turned his gaze to Brady. 'You ain't seen anythin' suspicious on the trail, have you?'

Brady shook his head. 'Nope.'

Ford looked across at Hayes, who diverted his perceptibly worried attention to Gibson.

'How about you?' Ford turned to him.

Hayes returned his gaze back to the marshal. 'What? No, nothing like that.'

Ford hipped in the saddle. 'Friends of yours, Gibson?'

Gibson stiffened a little but refused to look at Ford.

'Never seen 'em before,' he lied.

'Are you sure?'

Gibson ignored him.

'What do you plan on doin' with the bodies?' Hayes asked.

'I'll take 'em and plant 'em,' Ford told him. 'I was goin' to do that when I spied your wagon train. I thought I'd see if anybody from the wagon train knew who they were.'

'No one from this train knows 'em,' Hayes said

adamantly.

'I could just take 'em over. . . .'

'I said no one knows 'em, Marshal,' Hayes said impatiently. 'We got us women and children with the wagon train. They don't need a sight like this upsettin' 'em.'

Gibson's hand dropped to his gun butt which didn't go unnoticed. Ford shifted his gaze to Brady who'd done the same but his face remained passive in the face of growing tension. He looked back at Hayes.

'All right then, have it your way.'

Without another word, Hayes and Gibson started back towards the wagon train.

'Those two are mixed up in this somehow,' Ford stated.

Brady nodded. 'I think you're right. But the question is, what are they mixed up in?'

There was a brief silence between the two. The void was filled by the sound of the wind in the surrounding trees and oxen bawling their protest at the coming day.

'At least your cover is still intact,' Ford said.

'That's somethin',' Brady said. 'What about you? What are you goin' to do?'

'I'll be out there watchin' and waitin',' Ford told him. 'Though I don't think we'll have long to wait. Those two dead fellers were here for a reason. I think the next couple of days will tell the story.'

'I'd like to put a bullet in that son of a bitch's guts,' Gibson cursed as they walked back to the line of canvas covered wagons.

'You'll get your chance,' Hayes assured him. 'I have a

feelin' from now on, United States Marshal Josh Ford won't be too hard to locate.'

'What are we goin' to do now Pike and Cross are dead?'

'We'll have to do it ourselves,' Hayes informed him. 'This afternoon when you head out to find fresh meat for the train, find Ford and kill him.'

'What about Brady? Pike and Cross were meant to deal with him tonight while he was on watch. We'll reach the valley tomorrow.'

'We'll take care of him tonight. You just make sure you don't miss that marshal.'

Ford interred the two outlaws with all of their belongings then turned their horses loose.

Once finished, he went back to shadowing the wagon train.

For the rest of the morning and most of the afternoon, the landscape remained unchanged. A mix of tree-line ridges, clear water streams and verdant deep green meadows.

It was mid-afternoon when Ford found the signs of unshod horses. He examined the soft earth and made out five sets of tracks in all. The riders had stopped on the ridge.

Ford guessed that they'd watched the wagon train's approach, then moved on in the same direction of travel. He decided to cut across the wagon train's back trail and use the trees on the other side to continue. The last thing he needed was to run into a band of hostile Nez Perce.

41

He was halfway across when the whiplash of a Winchester cracked. His ears began to ring from the slug's glancing blow, so he knew that he'd been hit. His head started to spin and the far off sound of the shot broke through the haze. He was unable to retain his balance atop the blue roan. He leaned to the left and toppled from the saddle and landed in the knee high grass he'd been traversing.

The sun was low in the sky when Gibson rode into the wagon train camp with a young elk draped over the back of his horse. He left it with one of the immigrants to dress and went to find Hayes.

He found him at the wagon the two had acquired for the arduous journey. It was filled with mining supplies, shovels, picks, pans and such, all of which Hayes had purchased before they'd left Helena. Gibson was its main driver but when he was away, Hayes took over the reins.

'Did you find him?'

'Yeah. I took care of it.'

'Good.'

'There's a bunch of Nez Perce out there ridin' around, too,' Gibson informed Hayes.

'How many?'

'Not enough to worry us,' he answered. 'What about the scout?'

'We'll take care of it tonight,' Hayes said. 'Bend a gun barrel over his head and we'll truss him up and put him in the wagon.'

'Why not kill him?'

'Maybe the boss can use him.'

Gibson nodded and asked, 'What if these damned immigrants start givin' us trouble?'

'They won't,' Hayes spoke confidently. 'You'll see to that.'

CHAPTER 6

A sharp pain in Ford's shoulder brought him back from the depths of unconsciousness. He turned his head groggily and came face to face with what could be misconstrued as a smile on the mean-tempered blue roan that had just bitten him.

'Son of a bitch,' he cursed and lashed out at the horse's nose, rolling over onto his back.

Satisfied that it had done its job, the horse walked away a few yards and began to crop grass.

Pain ran through Ford's head. The dull throbbing ache made him feel nauseous. He opened his eyes and lay patiently as he waited for them to focus.

The first thing he noticed was the darkness. Overhead, the clear night sky held thousands of bright little pin-pricks of light which sparkled. The moon covered the landscape in a mantle of silver light.

Ford raised a hand to his head and gently probed the bullet furrow across his scalp. He was thankful to find it was quite shallow and not very wide. A very close call.

The world spun violently as he sat up slowly then

lurched to the side and emptied the contents of his stomach onto the grass. He lay back, closed his eyes and blackness claimed him, the harsh throbbing of his head mercifully blocked.

Brady felt uneasy. He knew something was up but couldn't put his finger on it. He sat beyond the wagon circle on an old stump with a Winchester rifle across his lap.

Maybe Ford was right. Perhaps something would happen in the next couple of days. Whatever it was.

The sound of footfalls behind him set Brady on edge. He thumbed back the hammer on his Winchester and turned from the waist to see who approached.

Hayes moved around to stand in front of him.

'All quiet?'

Brady nodded warily. 'So far, so good.'

'Just keep your eyes peeled,' Hayes ordered. 'There may be somethin' in what that marshal was sayin' earlier.'

Brady remained silent, he didn't have to be told.

'There was somethin' else today, too,' Hayes continued. 'When Gibson was out huntin' up some grub, he came across some unshod pony tracks. He's sure they were Nez Perce. Not many but enough to run off some stock.'

Brady sensed a movement behind him and whirled to bring the Winchester about. He was quick, but not quick enough.

A six-gun fell savagely and brought him to his knees. His ears rang and bright lights exploded in his head. Brady tried to rise to his feet but failed. The six-gun fell

again and he descended into the dark chasm of unconsciousness.

Ford knew what was about to happen even though he
was still in that foggy half state of not quite awake but no
longer asleep.

'Do it again and I'll shoot you.'

The roan snorted derisively and walked away a few
strides.

'Damn horse,' he groaned. 'Like I don't hurt enough
without you takin' another chunk out of my hide.'

The early morning sun had poked its orange head
above the eastern horizon and Ford opened his eyes to
have them assailed by the brightness.

He shut them tight, blinked a little then opened them
again. High in the morning sky, an eagle flew lazy circles
over what it thought was its next meal.

Ford was able to sit up without too much trouble. His
head still hurt but the pain had subsided a fraction. He
reached up and touched his blood encrusted scalp ten-
derly.

'Damn bushwhacker,' he cursed. 'When I catch up to
you, you'll wish you'd never been born.'

Ford dropped his hand to his hip and found the Colt
still there. Thank goodness for small mercies. Next, he
looked over at the horse. It seemed fine and his saddle
and Winchester were still there.

'Guess that means it wasn't Indians,' he said aloud
and the roan looked at him. 'Then again, maybe it would
have been better if it were.'

The roan snorted.

Ford's hat lay beside him and he picked it up and gingerly placed it on his head. He wobbled as he stood up, but soon gained some steadiness.

He looked about a full circle of the landscape but saw nothing that alarmed him.

'Come here, you,' he ordered the roan.

The animal looked up and decided on its next move. It walked casually over to Ford and waited for him to mount.

Ford climbed aboard and turned the animal down the valley. He wanted to find a stream to clean himself up in, then he intended to go after the wagon train.

'I can't seem to find him anywhere, Mr Hayes,' the middle-aged man said, perplexed. 'It's just like he disappeared.'

'We'll move out anyway, Reed,' Hayes said, a note of authority dissuading the man from further questions. 'Brady will just have to catch up.'

'Well, all right. Though travellin' without a scout out front in Indian country is a little disconcerting.'

'I'll send Gibson out,' Hayes said to allay his fears. 'He knows the trail.'

'Where is he? Come to think of it, I ain't seen him around this mornin', either.'

'Don't you worry none about Gibson. He's over in our wagon fixin' somethin' for me.'

Reed seemed satisfied with that and returned to his own wagon. Hayes went to the back of his and looked casually about to make sure nobody was looking, then drew the flap back marginally.

The compact space was no longer vacant but contained Gibson who held a six-gun to the head of a bound and gagged Brady.

'Is he givin' you any trouble?' Hayes asked.

'Him? Nope. I think he knows that I'll put a bullet in his brain if he does.'

Brady looked at Hayes and the wagon master saw only pure hatred. 'I think our friend here doesn't like us much, Matt.'

'He's goin' to like us less when we get where we're goin',' he chuckled.

'I need you out scoutin',' Hayes told Gibson. 'I told Reed that I'd send you out. At least that way it will keep him off our backs.'

'What about him?' Gibson said and pointed at Brady with his gun.

Hayes's eyes closed to slits as he looked menacingly at the governor's man. 'If he gives me any trouble, he's liable to have an accident.'

Gibson holstered his six-gun and climbed down from the back of the wagon.

'When you get to the pass, wait there for us,' Hayes ordered.

'Sure. I'll be there somewhere.'

Ford scooped sweet, cool water to his mouth from the stream where he knelt. A hundred yards to his left, it fed into a beaver pond made from felled aspen.

He cleaned his scalp wound carefully and washed up quickly, eager to get back on the trail and find the wagon train.

The roan snorted and stomped a hoof which caused Ford to drop his hand to his six-gun. He looked up to see five Nez Perce Indians emerge from a stand of tall firs on the far side of the valley.

Ford stood slowly but kept his eyes on the riders. He flicked the looped thong from the hammer of his Colt with his thumb and watched as the Indians approached.

Once they were close enough for Ford to see their horses clearly, he couldn't help but admire the magnificent beasts. In his opinion, there was no better sight than a Nez Perce horse.

They stopped line abreast on the opposite bank of the stream. All were armed and looked unhappy at his presence.

The big Indian in the centre spoke first.

'My name is Chuslum Moxmox,' he said in surprisingly good English. 'In your language, I'm known as Yellow Bull.'

'My name's Josh Ford,' Ford informed him.

Yellow Bull nodded. 'What brings you here, Josh Ford?'

'You know, we could yell back and forward across this stream until our voices grow sore or you can come over here where it would be easier to answer your questions.'

The Indian thought momentarily then nodded. He conferred briefly with his warriors, not loud enough for Ford to hear, then heeled his mount forward.

The animal splashed across the stream and up onto the bank. From there, Yellow Bull moved closer to Ford but remained on his horse.

He was a big man. Ford guessed that he was in his

early thirties and every bit of six foot two. Clad in buckskin pants and a vest which exposed his deep, powerful
chest and arms that rippled with muscle. A serious
expression looked to be permanent on the chiselled,
hawkish face and long, dark hair was held back by a
rawhide headband. He was armed with a .56 calibre
Spencer carbine.

Yellow Bull set his black eyes on Ford and repeated
the question. 'Why are you here, Josh Ford?'

'I'm a Deputy United States Marshal,' Ford started to
explain. 'I have been sent out here to investigate the disappearance of a number of wagon trains. I am ... was
trailing one when I was bushwhacked and left for dead.'

'Uh huh,' was all Yellow Bull said.

'You saw it happen?'

'Yes.'

'Why didn't you come and look at me?' Ford asked.

'Thought you dead,' Yellow Bull told him matter of
factly.

'Why didn't you steal my horse?' Ford said. 'If you
thought I was dead then. . . .'

Yellow Bull screwed up his face and grunted. 'Would
you steal him?'

Ford let it go then a thought came to him and he said,
'You were trailin' it, too? The wagon train. Why?'

'We watch many,' Yellow Bull told him. 'Some leave
our lands, others go into the valley, never return.'

Ford frowned. 'What valley?'

'We call it Valley of Thunder. Many times see wagons
go in. None come out.'

'Have you ever been in there?'

50

The big Indian shook his head. 'No. Place of bad spirits. Twice, send this many warriors into valley.'

Yellow Bull held up a hand and showed Ford five fingers.

'Of them, only one return. He die before next moon.'

'Did he say what he found?'

Yellow Bull shook his head. 'He dying. Only talk about four legged beast that attack him.'

Ford thought for a moment. He was certain that the wagon train was headed for that valley. But there was still hope with Brady.

He looked at Yellow Bull and said, 'Is that where the wagon train has gone?'

Yellow Bull shrugged his powerful shoulders. 'Maybe.'

'Can you show me where it is?'

Yellow Bull nodded. 'I show you.'

The big Indian turned his horse and called out to his companions. Their conversation ended and the four warriors swung their mounts away and galloped off.

'Where are they goin'?'

'Back to village,' Yellow Bull said. 'In valley of White River.'

Ford guessed that the big Indian's reference was to the Rapid River. It had been named by trappers because of its many rapids caused by its mainly rocky bottom.

'I guess we'd best be goin' then,' Ford said.

Yellow Bull looked at him, a grim expression on his stony façade. 'Do not be in hurry, Josh Ford. You too may never return from Valley of Thunder.'

CHAPTER 7

'But the trail goes that way,' Brian Ellis protested at the proposed change of route for the wagon train.

'He's right,' put in Reed, who pointed along the valley. 'The trail to Parsons is that way.'

'And I agree with you,' Hayes said. 'But Gibson came to me and informed me of a large war party of Nez Perce further on.'

'No, we should stick to the main trail,' Ellis said firmly. 'Goin' the way you propose could take us a week longer.'

'And it could also save your life and that of your wife,' Gibson remarked. 'Allison, too.'

Ellis's head snapped around, his eyes ablaze. 'Don't you dare speak my daughter's name. You ain't fit to.'

Throughout the trip, Gibson had made unwanted advances towards Allison Ellis and her father had had enough. He took a step towards Gibson but halted abruptly when Hayes's man drew his six-gun and eased back the hammer. His lined face paled then turned as ashen as the hair on his head.

'Take one more step, Ellis, and I'll gut shoot you,'

Gibson threatened. There was no anger in the killer's voice, just a cold, calculated tone of menace.

'Maybe they're right,' Reed said hurriedly, trying to defuse the situation. 'Maybe it will save us from an Indian attack. It can't hurt.'

Ellis nodded jerkily. 'All right, Hayes, we'll do it your way.'

The wagon boss smiled coolly. 'Get back to your wagons then. Once we get rollin', swing 'em right and follow the trail.'

Once they were gone, Hayes turned to Gibson, who still had his Colt drawn. 'Put it away, Matt.'

'I'm goin' to kill that feller.' Gibson scowled. 'You mark my words.'

'If you killed everyone you said you were goin' to, the boss would have no one left to do what he wants.'

Gibson scowled again. 'He's different.'

'Did you get word we were comin' in?' Hayes asked.

Gibson nodded. 'Yeah. They should be waitin' on the other side. Once we get through, Mills and the others will close in from behind.'

Hayes looked up into the sky. They had maybe five hours before the sun went down. 'Let's get 'em through. You lead out.'

From outside, the pass looked much like an opening in the ridge line filled with trees. Once inside, the walls grew into sheer grey rock faces with deep vertical scars.

The firs stood tall and thick but some had been cleared to allow sufficient space for a narrow wagon to wind its way through.

The combination of high walls and thick trees blocked the wind which created an echo effect for their voices that filtered through the trees in the stillness. It also contributed to a premature dimness which gave the pass a permanent twilight feel.

The wagons lumbered along the trail for a mile before it widened out into a small valley. It resembled a slice of paradise bordered on the left by a steep ridge and on the right, a towering granite cliff.

The valley had large tracts of silver-barked aspen, spruce, and lodgepole pines. A small beaver pond was fed from a large clear water lake which was fed by the snow melt each spring.

Once clear of the trees, the trail veered to the right, towards the granite cliffs. When the last wagon was through, Hayes called a halt to their progress. He climbed down from his wagon and walked a short way back along the line.

'What're we stoppin' for now?' asked Reed, perplexed.

Hayes nodded towards a large stand of larch. 'We're waitin' for them.'

Ten wraith-like figures on horseback emerged from the trees. All were armed with Winchester rifles.

Hayes turned and looked beyond Reed's wagon and said, 'Them, too.'

Reed looked around and saw the same happening on the right side. His heart lurched as fear gripped him. He sat down hard on the wagon seat beside his wife, his face ashen.

'Who . . . who're they?' he asked, not really wanting to

know the answer.

'They're friends of mine,' Hayes informed him.

There were muffled cries of alarm from a few of the settlers taken aback at the sudden appearance of the armed men.

Ellis paled, shocked at what was happening. When he regained his composure, he made a determined though unwise decision and fumbled for the rifle at his feet.

The sound of a gunshot echoed through the valley and Ellis stiffened as a bullet singed his cheek.

'The next one goes between your eyes,' said Gibson with a cold smile.

The two groups of riders closed in on the line of wagons which created an effective envelope.

'All right!' Hayes shouted. 'Get 'em off the wagons. They all walk from here.'

With loud protests, the wagon train people were forced from their conveyances and set afoot. Hayes went to the back of his wagon and climbed in. He took a knife and cut the bonds that secured Brady and said harshly, 'Get the hell out there and start walkin'.'

'Where are we?' Brady said.

'Just get out,' Hayes ordered. 'You'll see soon enough.'

Brady alighted from the wagon and was alarmed at the presence of the armed men. He turned full circle, and took in his surrounds, hoping that the landscape would provide some hint as to where they had been taken.

He frowned and repeated, 'Where the hell are we?'

*

'There is way into valley,' said Yellow Bull, who pointed out the tree-filled pass. 'Beyond trees, you find what you seek.'

Ford looked down at the churned up earth that signalled the direction change of the wagon train earlier in the day. The sun had gone down and he thought that the onset of darkness would help cover his approach so he decided to wait a little longer before trying to venture in.

'You wouldn't care to come with me, would you?' he asked Yellow Bull.

'Now you on your own,' the big Indian told him. 'Spirits angry enough without me go there.'

Ford nodded. 'I thought so.'

Yellow Bull's face took on a stern expression as he said to Ford, 'Goodbye, Josh Ford. I doubt I see you again.' With that, he swung his horse about and cantered off. Ford frowned and said aloud to nobody in particular, 'Thanks for the vote of confidence.'

Ford moved the roan off the trail and into some trees where he made a cold camp while he waited for night to fall. Ten minutes into his wait, he heard a far off rumble, not unlike thunder. Ford frowned. Though deep into the trees, he knew there were no clouds about.

The echo died away but left questions in the deputy marshal's mind. Whatever he found in the valley, he was certain that it would have nothing to do with spirits.

Brady was shoved unceremoniously into a dim, single room building similar to a small log cabin. He stumbled on the earthen floor but regained his balance and steadied himself.

Three log-width slits high up in the walls provided the only illumination for the space which was very little.

'Looks like another train has arrived,' a man's voice spoke from the gloom.

Brady tensed. 'Who's there?'

The figure of a man, clad in what could be classed as rags, moved haltingly into the almost non-existent light. He was unshaven and the growth on his face indicated that he had not done so in a long time. The smell emanating from him told Brady that he probably hadn't washed in that length of time, too.

'Who are you?' Brady asked him.

'My name is Finn,' the man answered in a dry voice. 'Thaddeus Finn.'

'Is there anyone else here with you?'

The man chuckled, a raspy sort of a sound that turned into a wracking cough. After he'd gathered himself, Finn said, 'If you mean in here, yes there's a few others. If you mean out there, then there's a whole lot more.'

'What is this place?' Brady asked, confused.

Finn gave another dry chuckle. 'Hell, son. You've just entered Hell.'

CHAPTER 8

The moon was fairly high when Ford decided it was time to move. He climbed up on the blue roan and moved out of the trees where he'd made his temporary camp.

The night air was cool but not cold. Up above in the blackened sky, the moon was surrounded by stars. Horse and rider crossed a small meadow lit by the pale silver of the moon above. Ford followed the wagon trail as it entered the trees and disappeared into the stygian darkness, blacker than the night.

'That's far enough, stranger,' the man ordered. 'Just raise them hands and keep 'em there. Don't make any sudden moves or I'll ventilate your hide.'

Ford cursed himself for his lack of caution. When he'd emerged from the pass, the last thing on his mind was a guard of sorts. The darkness had made him careless and complacent and now he was in trouble.

He raised his hands. 'Just hang on a minute there, mister. I ain't no trouble. Fact is, I'm lost.'

'You got that right,' the man allowed.

'I been ridin' around in circles for two days,' Ford

tried to bluff his way out of the situation. 'You're the first feller I've seen, apart from some Indians, that is.'

'What Indians?' the man snapped.

I don't know,' Ford lied. 'I didn't hang around long enogh to ask 'em. Say, what is this place anyway?'

'For you, trouble.'

The man fired his rifle three times into the air; orange flame sprouted from the end of the barrel.

'What was that about?' Ford asked him.

'Never you mind. Just climb on down from that nag of yours and take a seat.'

The roan snorted at the derisive reference.

'But before you do,' the man continued, 'get rid of that six-gun you got strapped on.'

Ford unbuckled the gun belt and let it fall to the earth. Then he climbed down and sat on the ground a few yards from the roan. 'What now?' he asked.

'We wait.'

He didn't have to wait long. Ten minutes later, he heard the drum of hoofbeats. Slowly they grew louder until two riders appeared out of the night. They drew up and asked the guard, 'What's goin' on, Mills?'

Ford recognized the voice instantly and his blood ran cold.

'He's just lettin' you know you've got a visitor,' he said.

The deputy marshal could see the rider's head snap about in the moonlight. 'Ford, is that you?'

'Yeah, Gibson, it's me.'

'Son of a bitch,' Gibson cursed loudly. 'You should be dead.'

'If you'd been a better shot I would be. Guess I was

59

lucky, you can't shoot for sh—'

'By hell I won't miss now,' Gibson snarled.

'Hold it, Matt!' the second rider cut in. It was Hayes.

'Where there's one you'll find the other,' Ford said.

'Let me shoot him, Hayes,' Gibson almost pleaded.

'No, we'll take him to the boss,' Hayes decided. 'He can figure out what to do with him.'

He turned to Ford. 'Get on your horse, Marshal. It's time to meet the Lord.'

The three of them drew up outside a long log cabin, complete with veranda. Lamplight shone through the windows and cast a dull yellow glow over the approaches to the entry.

Ford climbed down from the roan and was about to tie him to a sturdy hitch rail when Hayes stopped him.

'Matt, get rid of the horse,' Hayes ordered. 'Put him with all of the others.'

Gibson grumbled but did what he was told. As he walked off, Ford warned him, 'Be careful of him. He's a mule-headed, cantankerous son of a gun. And he'll try to nail you if you ain't careful. But you treat him good or I'll kill you.'

Gibson snorted contemptuously and led the horse away.

'Right,' said Hayes. 'Let's go and see the Lord. You lead.'

Ford swung the door open and was immediately taken aback by the quality of furnishings that decorated the large room of the cabin. Handmade, polished furniture, wall paintings, kerosene lamps, a lounge and a bear-skin rug on the timber floor in front of a blazing log fire-place.

The animal on that rug almost made Ford take a backward step. Especially when it stood up. It was a dog, though unlike any he'd seen before.

It had a grey, shaggy coat, stood somewhere over waist height and Ford estimated it weighed somewhere in the vicinity of 120-130 pounds.

With a deep guttural growl, it took a step towards him and made Ford freeze.

'Down, Caesar,' a voice snapped and Ford watched as the large canine settled back on the rug.

He felt the tension drain from him at that single movement.

'Quite something, isn't he?' commented the voice. This time, Ford could clearly recognize the accent as English.

'Yeah.' Ford nodded. 'He's somethin' all right.'

'He's an Irish Wolfhound. I brought him with me from England when I came to this uncivilized place four years ago. He was but a pup then.'

Ford dragged his gaze away from the dog and focussed upon the speaker.

The man had risen from a high-backed chair that fronted the fire. He stood facing them, backlit by the fire's orange glow.

Ford guessed he was forty-five or close to it. He stood a shade over six feet and his solid frame was well dressed in a tailored suit.

'My name is Lord Bruce Ferguson,' the man said in his heavily accented English. 'Welcome to my home. My valley in fact.'

'His name is Josh Ford, Lord Bruce,' Hayes introduced him. 'He's a United States Marshal.'

Ferguson frowned. 'I see. An officer of colonial law. We seem to have had an influx of policemen lately, Mr Hayes. First that other man and now Mr Ford. It would seem that someone outside of our world has taken an interest in our operation.'

'He's the feller that killed Pike and Cross,' Hayes informed his boss.

'I see.' Ferguson nodded grimly. 'The question is, what to do with you, Mr Ford.'

Ford remained silent.

'I think we'll put you to work until I decide,' Ferguson said. 'What do you think, Mr Hayes?'

'I'll see to it, Lord Bruce.'

'Nothing to say, Mr Ford?' the Englishman asked.

'Yeah.' Ford nodded. 'Who the hell are you?'

'I already told you. I am Lord Bruce Ferguson.'

Ford shook his head. 'No, there's more to it than that. Why would an English lord leave his country and come all the way out here to this "uncivilized country"? Your words, not mine. It don't add up to me. I think you're nothin' more than a common outlaw with an accent and no more relation to the British aristocracy than Hayes here. See, I know a few big words myself.'

Ferguson turned red as his rage built. There was silence as he fought to bring his ire under control and when he next spoke, it was measured and clipped.

'Put him with the others, Mr Hayes,' Ferguson ordered. 'I'll not stand in my own home and be insulted by a commoner such as this.'

Hayes grabbed Ford by the arm to lead him away when Ferguson stopped them both.

'One other thing, Mr Hayes. Tomorrow I think we'll show Mr Ford how we deal with insubordination. I think five cuts with the cat should suffice for a first offence.'

Hayes smiled coldly. 'I think so, Lord Bruce.'

'Good, it's settled,' Ferguson announced. 'And you, Mr Ford, once it's over, shall understand that there is only one law in this valley. Mine.'

Ford staggered as the rough hand propelled him forward through the door. He stumbled over something on the floor and crashed headlong into the far wall. All that prevented serious injury were his extended arms trying to arrest his fall.

Ford got up and cursed loudly then began to stumble back towards the closing door when he felt a hand on his shoulder.

'Easy there, young feller,' a voice from the darkness advised him. 'It won't do you any good.'

'Who's there?' Ford asked.

A new voice joined in. 'Is that you, Ford?'

'Brady?'

'Yeah, it's me,' the governor's man said.

'What the hell is this place?'

'I can tell you,' Brady said. 'But you ain't goin' to like it.'

'Try me.'

'Come over here and take a seat against the wall and I'll fill you in.'

Going more by feel than anything, Ford made his way to Brady and sat down and leaned against a solid wall. The cloying stench of many unwashed bodies hit him and took his breath away.

'How many people are in this building?' Ford said, covering his mouth and nose with his hand.

'As near as I can figure,' Brady told him, 'about ten.'

'What's it all about?'

'In one word, gold. The feller who runs this operation had himself a big old mine in a cliff face here somewhere and is usin' slave labour to dig it out.'

'I've met him,' Ford said and went on to tell Brady what had happened.

'From what I can gather, this Lord Bruce's floggin's are a regular occurrence,' Brady said. 'He once flogged a man to death for tryin' to escape. And another feller was hunted down usin' that damn dog of his.'

Ford's blood ran cold at the thought of being mauled by the big Irish Wolfhound.

'Tell me about the mine,' Ford said.

'I don't really know much about it.'

'I can tell you,' a voice said from the darkness.

'Who are you?' Ford said.

'His name is Thaddeus Finn,' Brady said. 'He's one of those who's been here the longest. Finn, this is Josh Ford. He's the man I was tellin' you about.'

'Uh huh.'

'How long?' Ford asked.

'As near as I can figure, about three years,' Finn answered. 'I was the first. Some of the ones who came after me are long dead. Worked to death in the mine.'

'Has he been taking slaves for that long?' said Ford, amazed.

'Yeah,' Finn said. 'At first, he started with drifters, prospectors and the like. He used a few Indians, too. The deeper the mine went, the more workers he needed. And more men to guard them. Then he came up with the wagon train idea.'

Ford thought for a moment and said aloud, 'If he hadn't started taking the wagon trains, no one would have been the wiser to his operation in this valley.'

'That's what greed will do to you,' Finn said. 'The more he has, the more he's wanted. He was bound to slip up sooner or later. I just wish it had been sooner.'

'What does he do with the gold?'

'He waits until he has enough and it goes out by mule train.'

Ford frowned. Yellow Bull never mentioned anything about mule trains.

'How do they get them out?' Ford enquired.

'There is another way out,' Finn explained. 'Only accessible by the mules and horses. A wagon can't make it.'

'So where does it all go?'

'He ships it to Seattle. Word is he has another man on that end who stores it.'

'How do you know all this, Finn?'

'I got ears. I hear things.'

'What about the women and children?' Ford asked. 'What happens to them?'

'Everybody works in the mine,' Finn's voice grew harsh. 'Men, women, and children. Except for a select few who cook and clean and ... and entertain the guards.'

'Bastards,' Brady cursed.

'How many guards?'

'Approximately thirty of 'em, give or take.'

'What are we goin' to do, Ford?' Brady said. 'Any ideas?'

'Get through tomorrow to start with,' Ford said. 'And after that, who knows. However, one thing is for sure. I ain't stayin' here and neither are these people.'

CHAPTER 9

The door to the log prison flew back with a crash and let in a stream of blinding sunlight. As two men entered and filled the doorway, they blocked most of the light.

'Everyone out,' a man ordered. 'Now.'

With a few moans and muffled curses, the filth ridden prisoners climbed to their feet and shuffled towards the door. The two guards moved aside to allow them to pass.

Ford and Brady joined the end of the procession and as they exited their cell, the two men grabbed Ford by the arms.

'You come with us,' one of them snarled. 'Everybody gather over at the scaffold.'

Ford had resigned himself to what was going to happen. To be able to escape, he needed to get through it and work out a plan from there. Therefore, when the two men led him away, he didn't even struggle.

They took him to what could have been classed as a parade ground. A large square patch of earth was long devoid of grass, surrounded by log huts, and at its centre stood a triangular scaffold, a rope dangling from its apex.

Ferguson stood to the left, impeccably dressed and immaculate in his suit. He smiled coldly, his dog by his side. 'Tie him to the scaffold ready for punishment to be carried out,' he ordered. 'Learn from this, Mr Ford. It may benefit you in the future.'

Ford ignored the autocrat's statement and let his gaze wander over the gathered crowd. Men, women, and children. They were all there. All looked beaten and downtrodden. Clothes were dirty and ripped beyond repair.

The new arrivals, however, stood out in stark contrast with their clean apparel amongst the sea of filth. Their faces were masks of fear and confusion.

Ford was forced to remove his shirt and could feel the pricks of the early morning chill on his exposed skin.

Then the two men tied Ford roughly to the scaffold, arms raised above his head.

'I'm goin' to enjoy this,' Gibson whispered harshly into his ear. 'I just wish it was more than five.'

Ford turned his head to face the outlaw. Gibson's smile was full of mirth.

'Just so you know, Gibson,' Ford said matter of factly, 'I'm goin' to kill you before this is all done.'

The marshal let his hard gaze linger on Gibson's face and for a moment, he thought he caught a glimpse of fear in the killer's eyes. Fleeting though it was, Gibson gave him one last flinty smile then walked around behind Ford.

Ferguson then stepped forward to address the gathered crowd.

'Those of you who have been with us for a while will

know by now that I will not tolerate insubordination of any kind,' he started. 'Those of you who are new, take heed from what you are about to witness. This is what happens when you colonials decide to ignore the rules that are in place. Prepare yourself, Mr Ford, for you are about to feel the kiss of the Captain's Daughter.'

Ferguson looked across at Gibson who waited patiently for the signal with cat in hand. He nodded and Gibson stepped forward for the first lash.

The cat o' nine tails as it was known throughout the English armed services was crudely fashioned from a length of wood and cotton cords plaited together. Knots were tied at the end of each two and a half foot strand.

Ford frowned thoughtfully. Navy men had another name for it. The Captain's Daughter.

His thoughts were quickly replaced by lightning bolts of pain behind his eyes with the burn of the first lash of the cat. The resounding crack of the tails on bare flesh echoed across the punishment ground.

'One!' Ferguson shouted loudly.

Ford bit back the cry that emanated deep in the back of his throat.

The lash whistled through the air again, telegraphing its arrival. The knots bit deep into Ford's skin. This time, a small gasp escaped his lips.

'Two!'

On the third, a louder gasp and in addition to the burning fire on his back, Ford could feel the blood start to run.

The fourth lash made his legs tremble but still there was no outburst or cry of pain. The fifth and final lash landed amongst the blood and torn flesh of Ford's back but he refused to give Gibson the satisfaction of a vocal cry. Beads of pain-induced sweat ran down the marshal's brow and dripped from his nose into the dirt at his feet.

The two men who had tied Ford to the scaffold now took him down. They supported his weight until he gathered himself then they left him to stand by himself.

In staccato movements, Ford turned until he faced Gibson, who still held the blood-spattered cat.

'What are you lookin' at?' Gibson hissed.

Through all of his burning pain, Ford managed a smile. A cold, hate-filled smile. When he spoke, it was low and menacing and sent a chill down the killer's spine.

'I'm lookin' at a dead man,' he said, just loud enough for Gibson to hear.

Gibson snarled and raised the cat to lash out at Ford but was stopped short.

'Mr Gibson!' Ferguson's voice cracked. 'That will be enough. Punishment is over.'

'Yes, sir, Lord Bruce.' Gibson scowled.

'Mr Hayes. See to it that Mr Ford gets put to good use. Have someone take care of those wounds first. I'd hate for him to get an infection and die before we've finished with him.'

'I'll fix him up, Lord Bruce,' said Finn as he stepped forward.

'I'll help him,' put in Brady.

Ferguson nodded. 'Very well. See to it, Mr Hayes, and then come see me in my quarters.'

'Yes, Lord Bruce.'

While the others dispersed, Brady and Finn helped Ford over to the shade of a tall tree and lay him face down on the grass.

'I'll be back in a moment,' Finn said as he turned and walked over to Hayes.

'How bad is it?' Ford asked.

'Looks a lot worse than it is,' Brady assured him.

'Hurts like hell,' Ford told him.

'This will hurt a lot more,' Finn said on his return.

'What is it?' said Brady as he looked at the small pouch in the man's hand.

'It's salt,' he informed them both. 'I'll put it on the wounds. Like I said, it'll hurt like hell, but it will stop any infection.'

'Get it done,' Ford said through gritted teeth.

Finn looked over at Brady. 'Hold him down.'

'You wanted to see me, Lord Bruce?'

'Yes, Mr Hayes,' Ferguson said. 'When will the next shipment for the mule train be ready to leave?'

'Maybe four days,' Hayes told him.

Ferguson nodded and walked over to stand by the open fireplace. He stood there in silence, deep in thought.

'I want you to delay it for another week to ten days.'

'But why?'

'I believe that our position here is rather tenuous,' Ferguson explained. 'First, we had that other man snooping around and now we have a Deputy United States Marshal in our midst. It is my opinion that it will not be long before a lot more, possibly a troop of cavalry, come looking. Before that happens, I want to get as much gold out as possible.'

Hayes couldn't believe his ears. 'But what if they come before then?'

'I suggest that we post lookouts along the trail, five miles out. That should give us fair warning.'

Hayes nodded. 'Is that all you require me for?'

'Yes, I think so.'

'I'll see to it straight away,' Hayes said and left the room.

'Well, this is it,' Finn announced.

Ford and Brady stopped and surveyed the large granite rock face in front of them and the large hole at its base.

'Not quite as big as I envisaged it to be,' Ford said.

'Nope,' Brady agreed. 'Why then do they need so many people to work a small mine like this?'

'You see, it's bigger than it looks. The main seam branches inside,' Finn told them. 'It splits three ways. Up until that point, you could obtain the gold real easy. But after it branches, you can mine all day and get pitiful amounts.'

Ford watched the enslaved civilians come and go from the mouth of the mine. The exiting workers bent double under the weight of their loads.

'We blast every second day then they take the rock about a hundred yards that way,' Finn said and indicated in the direction the workers travelled. 'There's a small creek where they wash the rock and sort out the ones with the gold in them.'

Ford's back was starting to stiffen and he doubted that he would be much use for the work crew that day. He stretched it and instantly regretted the move as pain shot in small jolts from the shredded tissue.

'Once we get inside,' Finn explained, 'we'll find you a place where you can rest up. Your back should be fine for you to work tomorrow since we put that salt on it.'

'Where did you get the idea of the salt anyway?' Ford asked him as he recalled the way it had burned on application.

Finn shrugged. 'It's somethin' we've always done. Ever since I can remember. His Lordship told us to do it after the very first flogging here. We've been doin' it ever since.'

Ford remained silent while he processed the snippet of information he'd been given.

Inside the mine, it was dusty, dim and odorous. The rough-hewn walls had jagged edges and lanterns cast their sickly glow. The enclosed space was rank with the smell of quiet despair and unwashed bodies. As they proceeded deeper into the shaft, people brushed past with their heavy loads. Their hopeless faces, anonymous masks of dust, grime and sores.

They reached the drive branch and took the left fork. Another fifty yards brought them to an abrupt halt as they were confronted with a solid mass of rock.

Ford found an out of the way spot to sit while the others went to work with picks on the rock face. The debris was scooped back behind them and shovelled into sacks to be carried out by the porters.

'Hey, Thaddeus,' Ford called to Finn, who leaned on his pick for a brief rest from his exertions. 'How come there ain't no guard up here?'

'They don't need one. A guard will look in every now and then but we're not exactly goin' anywhere, are we?'

'Nope,' Ford said. 'I suppose not. You don't happen to know how Ferguson came across this strike, do you?'

'Him.' Finn snorted in disgust. 'That damn son of a bitch couldn't find his nose even if he had a mirror and it was pointed out to him.'

'What in hell is that supposed to mean?'

'It means that he didn't find it,' Finn explained. 'It's my damned mine. The bastard took it from me.'

CHAPTER 10

The slaves worked steadily all day without rest. When evening finally arrived, the procession of bone weary, filthy bodies evacuating the mine was akin to ants leaving their colony on a frosty morning. Their shuffling feet carried them automatically to their cells for their meagre evening ration.

Supper was a watery broth with questionable green flotsam. On closer inspection, the protein content of the meal was nothing more than fat white maggots.

Ford tossed his bowl on the ground in disgust and Brady followed suit.

'I ain't gonna drink that damn swill,' Ford grated. 'I'll go to hell before I eat anythin' like that.'

'But you must eat,' Finn insisted as he picked out a plump larvae. 'If you don't, you won't last long.'

'I won't be here long enough to worry about going any distance,' Ford whispered harshly. 'I'm gettin' out.'

'When? How?' Finn seemed genuinely shocked that

anyone would contemplate such a rash move. 'Those who tried before you failed. Some even died. It is impossible.'

'Tomorrow. At the end of the day,' Ford started to explain. 'When we come out of the mine, I'll slip away into the brush—'

'Ah, make that we,' Brady interjected.

Ford stared at him then nodded. 'We. We'll hide out until dark then we do what we can to get out.'

'The guards will see you if you try to escape from the mine,' Finn pointed out.

'Well then, we'll need a distraction,' Brady stated.

Ford looked intently at Finn. 'Can you organize something for us?'

The man was hesitant at first, but after some thought, he nodded. 'I think so. But even if this crazy idea works, what will you do? It is at least a hundred miles to the nearest help.'

'Help may be closer than you think,' Ford said and went on to elaborate when both men gave him quizzical looks.

'I plan to head for the Nez Perce camp on the Rapid River,' Ford told them. 'Yellow Bull said that he and his people are there. If I can convince him that the valley isn't full of bad spirits, we might just have a chance.'

'Do you think he'll believe you?' Brady asked doubtfully.

'I guess we'll find out if and when we get there.'

Finn shook his head resignedly. 'This is a bad idea.'

'Maybe so,' Ford said. 'But it's the only one we have.'

The sound of raised voices drifted across the weary

gathering and all three men looked to see what was happening.

The first person Ford spied was Gibson. The man confronting the sadistic brute was someone Ford didn't recognize.

'Damn it,' Brady cursed softly.

'Well, you obviously know that feller,' Ford said.

'Yeah, that's Ellis. He's the feller I told you about that was havin' trouble with Gibson harassin' his daughter Allison.'

'Looks like he's been at it again then,' Ford said.

Before either of them could move, the situation rapidly escalated from bad to deadly.

Gibson grabbed the arm of a pretty young woman with blonde hair. Ford guessed that she was the man's daughter and the subject of Gibson's unwanted advances. She had placed herself between the two men in an attempt to calm her father and prevent a situation that may get him killed. Her efforts were to no avail. The instant Gibson grabbed her by the arm, Ellis launched himself, like a rabid snarling beast at the outlaw.

Gibson staggered back as Ellis careened into him, claw-like hands reached for his throat. Gibson was forced to let go of the young woman's arm to defend himself.

Reflexively, he clubbed Ellis' arms to one side with his left fist and his right snaked out. As Ellis staggered backwards under the onslaught, the blow only clipped him and had no impact on the enraged man.

Off balance, Gibson's feet tangled and he went down. Ellis threw himself atop the fallen outlaw and fixed his hands in a vice-like grip around his throat and began to squeeze the breath out of his assailant.

Two muffled shots rang out and Ellis stiffened then went limp, all fight extinguished.

Gibson rolled the dead man off, two patches of scarlet exposed on the man's chest, a still smoking six-gun in the outlaw's hand. Somehow, in the struggle, he'd managed to get it loose and discharge it with deadly efficiency.

The blonde woman screamed and dropped to her knees beside the body of Ellis.

'Hell,' snarled Brady and went to move forward.

Ford put out an arm to restrain him and said, 'Wait.'

Brady opened his mouth to protest but changed his mind and snapped it shut.

Gibson dragged himself to his feet, holstered his gun and brushed himself off. He stepped over to where the young woman wept over the body of her dead father.

She looked up at him with hate in her eyes. Tears streamed down her cheeks as she wept openly.

She spat at him and hissed, 'Damn you to hell, you murderer.'

Gibson smiled a cold, yellowed toothed smile, reached down and took a fistful of hair, then dragged her to her feet.

The young woman cried out in pain and kicked savagely at her father's killer. Her fists drummed out a staccato beat on Gibson's chest but he laughed maniacally and dragged her close.

'Ford,' Brady snapped. 'Are we just goin' to stand here and watch this?'

'Nope.' Ford shook his head. 'I'd say not.'

Both of them hurried towards the still laughing Gibson and his struggling prisoner.

'Let her go, Gibson,' Ford ordered.

The laugh stopped instantly and Gibson's face changed colour as he turned to meet his challenger. When he realized who had spoken, his face fell even further.

'Well, well,' he started, menace evident in his tone. 'If it ain't the marshal. Guess what, Ford? You don't get to tell me what to do here.'

Gibson dragged the woman closer and forced a kiss upon her. He looked back at the two men and smiled, the dare to them obvious.

'See. Here, I do what I want.'

Ford moved closer to Gibson and stood an arm's length from him. He glared into the man's eyes and said quietly, 'Let the woman go. Now.'

Once more, Gibson's face turned a reddish hue as his anger built.

'Why you!' he snarled and shoved the young woman to the ground.

His hand immediately dropped to the holstered six-gun but Ford reacted quickly and moved in closer. With his left hand, he chopped down onto the wrist of Gibson's gun arm. The outlaw cried out in pain and his hand went numb and the gun fell into the dirt at his feet.

Ford's right hand streaked out with the speed of a striking rattler and his closed fist hit Gibson flush in the mouth.

Ford felt the wounds on his back break open with the exertion of the violent reaction but he was satisfied when

Gibson went down hard.

The killer shook his head to clear his vision then wiped at his mouth with the back of his hand. It came away red with blood and he spat a globule into the dirt beside him.

With a loud snarl, Gibson lunged for the fallen Colt but as his hand closed about the walnut grip, a shout stopped him cold.

'Gibson, stop!'

Ford turned to look at the large figure of Hayes as he emerged from the front row of the gathered crowd.

'Leave it where it is, Matt,' Hayes said, 'and tell me what the hell is goin' on.'

'I'm about to kill me a lawman is what's goin' on,' Gibson said.

'Looks to me like you've already done enough killin' for one day,' said Hayes as he indicated Ellis' corpse on the ground.

'He should have minded his own business,' Gibson said.

'You were about to force yourself upon his daughter,' Brady pointed out.

'You shut up,' Gibson spat caustically. 'No one asked you.'

Hayes bent down and picked up Gibson's Colt. He stuck it in his belt then looked hard at the killer.

'Get 'em locked away then bury the body,' he commanded.

'The hell . . .' Gibson started.

'Just do it!' Hayes barked.

Gibson nodded stiffly then turned away. 'All right, you

lot. Get inside.'

Hayes turned his attention to Ford. 'Any more trouble from you and I'll shoot you myself.'

Ellis' daughter gave Ford and Brady a pitiful look as she was helped to her feet. She mouthed the words, 'Thank you,' and was guided away to her prison for the night.

'I'm goin' to kill that son of a bitch,' Brady seethed.

'You'll have to join the line,' Ford said. 'Because I already promised him that.'

CHAPTER 11

Throughout the following day, both Ford and Brady managed to rest as much as they could without drawing too much attention to themselves. They would require all the energy and stamina they could muster if they were to be successful in their escape attempt.

On approach to the mouth of the mine at the end of the day, Ford asked Finn, 'Are you ready?'

The man nodded. 'Just don't get caught.'

'We'll do our best,' Ford assured him.

There were three guards at the exit to the mine. Each one watched and counted to make certain the number that had gone in that morning equalled those coming out.

A few of the slaves carried bags of ore, Finn included. As he walked past a guard, he staggered under the bag's weight. A little at first, then he lost balance and crashed into the unsuspecting man which caused both of them to go down in a tangle of arms and legs.

The ensuing commotion of shouts, curses, and laughter from the remaining guards created enough distraction, and Ford and Brady slipped into the brush unseen.

The downed guard extracted himself from Finn and climbed to his feet. He lashed out with his boot.

'Damned old fool, why don't you watch where you're goin'?'

Finn managed to get to his feet and he picked up the bag once more and continued on his way.

'Damn it,' one of the guards cursed.

'What's up?' asked another.

'I damn well lost count.'

The guard shrugged. 'Don't worry about it. They're all there.'

Little did he know, but those words would come back to haunt him.

Ford and Brady moved swiftly through the trees until they found a place amongst some rocks and spruce to hide.

'What do you think?' Brady asked Ford as he caught his breath.

'So far, so good. If we can remain out of sight until dark, that will even things up a little and we'll stand a better chance.'

'Wish we had a couple of broncs,' Brady pondered.

Ford thought briefly about the roan. He hated to leave such a good horse behind but he knew that if all went well, he'd be back.

'We can't risk it,' he told Brady.

He nodded in acceptance. All they could do now was wait and hope that no one noticed their absence.

*

When the front door burst open, the huge Irish Wolfhound leapt to his feet from the bearskin rug in front of the fire. A low growl rumbled from deep within his throat and he bared his teeth at the intruder.

Darkness had fallen and Ferguson was seated at a large wooden table for his supper of venison and beans, a repast prepared by a widow of an emigrant long dead.

The fork stopped halfway to his mouth and he glared at the interloper who wore an alarmed expression.

'What is it, Hayes?' he demanded, resentful of the interruption.

'We have a problem,' Hayes answered. His lack of formality didn't go unnoticed. 'Ford and the scout, Brady, have gone.'

Ferguson calmly placed the fork onto his plate, retrieved the napkin from his lap, and wiped his mouth. He stood and leaned forward, braced himself with his fists pressed onto the tabletop.

'How?' The question was low and full of menace.

'I don't know.' Hayes shrugged his broad shoulders. 'I've got men organized to look now. But it will be full dark soon and that could prove a problem. In saying that, they couldn't have gone far.'

'I see,' Ferguson said in the same tone. 'Tell them to take Caesar and find them. And they are not to come back until they bloody well have!'

Ferguson bellowed the last part of the sentence and spittle flew from his lips as his rage erupted.

'If they make it out of the valley, there is no telling

84

who they could come across. If it's a cavalry patrol, we would be in no end of trouble. So I say again, tell them don't rest until they have them.'

Hayes nodded.

Ferguson looked down at his dog. 'Caesar. Hunt.'

The huge canine stood up and moved towards the door. Hayes opened it and allowed the dog to lead him out.

'Come on, keep moving,' Ford urged Brady. 'If we stop, we're done for.'

Behind them, their pursuers were gaining ground as they crashed through the trees. Ford figured they weren't far from the pass which had brought them into the valley.

The pair had been on the run and hiding out for the past few hours. With the addition of Ferguson's dog to the hunt, the men who chased them were now close behind.

Ford and Brady had been flushed from their hiding spot just before dark amid a flurry of gunfire but they'd managed to escape.

Darkness for the past couple of hours made things marginally better but the danger of being seen was replaced by the perils of what they couldn't see.

At one point, Brady had cannoned into a tree, which had opened up a cut on his cheek and given him an aching head. Though the moon was up and cast a silvery glow across the valley, the trees blocked most of its limited illumination.

From the shadows stepped the figure of a man.

'What the hell is goin' on?' he called to them as they approached. He'd assumed that they were friendly. 'What was all that gunfire I heard earlier?'

Ford dropped his shoulder and crashed headlong into the man. There was a loud grunt as the air whooshed from the guard and both he and Ford spilled to the damp ground.

They rolled around, clawing at each other until Ford gained the upper hand. The marshal drove a fist into the guard's face and there was an audible crunch as the man's nose broke in a spurt of blood.

He howled in pain and threw his head to one side. Ford slammed another punch into the injured man's face. The cries ceased and movement stopped as unconsciousness claimed him.

'Find his rifle,' Ford said to Brady as he relieved the outlaw of his six-gun and belt.

Brady scratched around until he found the Winchester dropped by the man when Ford had cannoned into him.

With heavy breaths from his exertions, Ford strapped on the man's gun belt and adjusted it until it was comfortable.

The night was rent with the sound of a blood-curdling howl which caused both men to freeze.

'Somehow I don't think that was a wolf,' Brady said.

'Nope,' Ford agreed. 'And I don't plan on hangin' around until it gets here, neither. That damn thing scares the hell out of me.'

'What? You, scared?'

'Just shut up and start runnin' if you don't want to

end up on its blamed menu.'

As the noise of the chasers behind them grew louder, Ford and Brady disappeared into the darkness of the tree-choked pass.

'We're getting' close now,' one of the pursuers called out after the wolfhound's howl had died away.

The hunters numbered four. All were on foot because they found it easier when working with the dog. Their names were Cook, Bell, Jordan, and Venters, and all of them were cold-hearted killers. This was the job they'd been recruited for.

Cook fought to hold Caesar back as he pulled hard against a long leash which could be easily unclipped as required.

The dog stopped suddenly and looked at a prone form in front of it. Confused, Cook moved forward to stand beside the dog. With some trouble, he could make out the body through the darkness.

'Son of a bitch,' Cook cursed loudly.

'What is it?' Jordan asked.

'It's Blake,' Cook told them. 'The bastards have killed him.'

A low moan came from the guard as he stirred slightly.

'Wait, he's still alive,' Venters said.

'Leave him be,' Cook ordered. 'We'll get him on the way back.'

Cook leaned down and unclipped the wolfhound's leash. 'Go on, boy, hunt.'

They watched the dog power off ahead, a large drab, grey streak against a silvery background.

*

The two exhausted men lumbered from the tree-line on tired legs. Before them lay the vast expanse of grassland that ran both sides of the wagon trail. On the far side was a low tree-clad ridge, not much bigger than a hill.

'We need to get across that before they come out behind us,' Ford said. 'Do you think you can make it?'

'Do you?' Brady shot back. 'You know, we could make a stand. We do have guns and some ammunition.'

'That's what I plan on doin',' Ford told him. 'Once we get across to the trees we'll be able to catch them out in the open. It'll still be dark but hopefully light enough to see them comin'.'

'What're we waitin' around here for then?' Brady asked as he broke into a lumbering run.

Ford followed close behind and they'd gone about halfway when a patch of uneven ground brought Brady down with a yelp of pain.

'Come on,' Ford urged him and grabbed a handful of clothing to help him to his feet. 'We ain't got no time to be rollin' around in the tall grass.'

'I'm done,' Brady gasped. 'I hurt my ankle. It's bad, I felt somethin' give and now it's burnin' like a bitch.'

'Get up,' Ford said as he dragged him upright with strength fuelled by adrenaline. 'I ain't leavin' you.'

Brady tried to put weight on his injured ankle but his whole leg buckled beneath him and he slumped to the ground. He gritted his teeth against the pain and hissed an inaudible curse.

'Leave me,' he said, giving voice to the only sensible

solution to their predicament. 'I got me a rifle. I can hold 'em off long enough for you to get away. Get help for the others.'

Ford surprised Brady when he sat down beside him.

'What the hell are you doin'?' he asked incredulously.

'When I was a boy,' Ford began, ignoring the question, 'we had us a mountain lion that came down outta the hills and killed one of our two milk cows. I was thirteen at the time. Pa was gone so it was just me, Ma and my older sister left there. Now, I got it into my head that the damn thing was goin' to come back and kill the other cow. Bein' poor folks as we were, we just couldn't afford to be buyin' another. So I took down my pa's old shotgun and sat outside every night, all night, for the next five nights.'

Ford paused a moment before he continued. 'Come that fifth night, my ma said to me, "Joshua, you know that cat ain't comin' back". Anyway, I just ignored her and went outside to wait again. As I was closin' the door behind me I heard her say, "Stubborn is what you are, Joshua Ford". Come mornin' I had that big cat. But my ma was right about one thing. I am damn stubborn and like I said before, I ain't leavin' you.'

Brady just shook his head.

Out of the darkness came the same blood-curdling howl they'd heard earlier.

'Better get ready,' Ford said. 'We're about to have company.'

CHAPTER 12

Ford and Brady crouched low in the grass, guns at the ready. Though faint, they could hear noises getting closer. A soft thrum on the earth was probably the stride of the giant wolfhound headed towards them. It was quieter than a horse but loud enough to be heard. From the rear, the shouts of the hunters grew steadily louder.

They rose up just enough to get a better view of the situation. The first thing they saw was the dog as it bounded towards them. Behind it, they could just make out the faint silhouettes of the men.

Ford returned his focus to the dog. It was their main threat and needed to be killed first.

The drumming of its paws grew louder as it got closer.

Both men raised their firearms and drew a bead on the approaching beast. Hammers went back with a dry triple-click that sounded unbelievably loud in the crisp night air.

The dog seemed to be so close, a beast sent from hell to hunt and kill its prey. Prey in this instance was Ford and Brady.

In a cruel twist of fate, as the wolfhound closed the distance between them to forty feet, the moon went behind a cloud and everything went black.

Orange stabs of flames sparked brightly in the darkness, followed quickly by the slap of multiple gunshots as Ford and Brady fired wildly. The four outlaws dived for cover as bullets passed close, loud crackles signalled their paths.

Venters, a little slower than the others, gave out a strangled cry as one of the wildly fired rounds found a mark.

'Who's hit?' Cook called out.

'Venters,' Jordan shouted back.

The other three opened fire at the muzzle flashes opposite them. Their guns thundered loudly as they unleashed a flurry of their own at those opposite.

'They were waitin' for us, with guns,' Bell yelled out. 'How the hell did they get guns?'

Cook recalled Blake, the unconscious guard they'd found back at the pass. He was about to voice his opinion when over the din of the shots, he heard a faint cry of pain when one of the guns opposite ceased fire, then the other.

'Hold your fire,' Cook ordered.

There was a loud yelp of pain followed by two gunshots then an all encompassing silence, save the heavy breaths of the three outlaws who remained belly down in the grass.

'Was that what I think it was?' Jordan asked in a harsh whisper.

'Yeah,' Cook growled. 'They got the dog. They got Caesar.'

91

*

'How's the arm?' Ford asked as he thumbed fresh loads into the six-gun.

'It hurts,' Brady complained. 'Good thing I managed to get it up, though, otherwise that damned beast would have taken my throat out.'

When the moon had disappeared behind the clouds and darkness had shrouded them, the pair had fired blindly in the general direction of the approaching dog in hope of stopping it dead.

All those shots had missed. The dog, that is. They had no idea that a stray bullet had taken down one of their pursuers.

When the snarling beast had come out of the darkness virtually on top of Brady, he'd had just enough time to throw up his forearm in a protective gesture.

The force of the impact had knocked Brady onto his back with the wolfhound still attached to his arm. The beast had then stood over him; a rumbling growl emanated from deep in its chest.

At first, Brady had cried out with pain but soon forgot the agony as he engaged in a life or death battle with the massive animal.

Ford had ceased fire and leapt to help the man in a struggle for his life. He used his six-gun as a club and it rose and fell twice. With the second blow, the dog yelped loudly and released Brady's arm. He then whirled on Ford to confront the new threat.

As Caesar leapt at Ford, the deputy marshal fired twice. The dog shuddered under the impact of the

92

bullets then crashed to the ground at Ford's feet.

In the silence that ensued, the pair waited and listened to the night sounds for any indication of the approaching men.

'What do you think?' Brady asked Ford.

Ford shrugged. 'I don't know. Maybe they're waitin' to see what we're goin' to do.'

They waited a few minutes more but nothing happened.

'Let's move, Brady,' Ford said as he helped him to his feet. 'We'll put some distance between us and them before daylight or they figure we ain't here.'

Whether by some quirk of fate or pure dumb luck, the night split apart once more with gunfire and the three outlaws appeared from the darkness. Somehow they'd managed to approach without a sound.

Ford palmed his six-gun and fired at the nearest silhouettes. He felt it buck in his palm as it sent slug after slug at the attackers. With satisfaction, he saw one of them disappear.

Beside him, Brady worked the lever of the Winchester and managed to get three shots off before the rifle's hammer fell on an empty chamber. As he struggled to reload, a bullet ploughed into his chest and another into his middle.

The governor's man grunted with the impact of each bullet. The empty rifle fell from his grip and he buckled at the knees before he sank slowly to the ground.

Ford felt the burn of a bullet as it fanned his face and another tugged at his pant leg. There was one shooter left and he had, by his calculations, two slugs remaining.

He was aware that Brady was down and knew that if he couldn't put the last attacker down with one of his final two shots, he'd be in dire trouble.

Calmly, he steadied the gun, took careful aim and fired his final two shots. The man in front of him fell back as both slugs hit him full in the chest.

Ford went down on one knee and reloaded. Once the loading gate was snapped shut, he paused and listened for any indication of more attackers out there in the darkness.

His ears were greeted by nothing more than night sounds.

He moved quickly to check on Brady. He knelt beside him to see if he was breathing. He was too late. There was nothing, the man was dead.

Ford muttered a curse under his breath. This was just one more reason to bring Lord Bruce Ferguson and his band of ruthless killers to justice.

He felt around the ground for the Winchester. He cracked it open and found it empty.

'Guess the six-shooter will have to do,' Ford said to nobody in particular. 'Shame them fellers didn't have horses.'

He looked across at Brady's still form. 'I'm sorry, Brady, but I ain't got time to bury you proper. I'll see to it when I get back. That's a promise.'

Without another word, Ford turned away, headed for the ridge line and hoped like hell he could find the help he required to liberate the slaves of the Valley of Thunder.

*

Mid-morning the following day saw Ford enter a broad valley with large tracts of larch and spruce. A shallow, swift-flowing stream allowed him to slake his thirst.

It also gave him cause for concern. Beside the stream, in a bare patch of earth, he found fresh signs of a large grizzly.

Instantly on edge, Ford scanned his surroundings a full 360 degrees. He had no desire to come across a bear with only a six-gun and no horse.

Relieved to find no further indication of the bear, Ford crossed the stream and kept on track for Rapid River and the Nez Perce camp.

An hour later, however, they found him. Ford looked up to see six of them. They sat atop their fine horses on a bald knoll and watched his very slow progress.

With loud cries, they urged their horses forward and thundered down the slope towards the virtually helpless man.

Ford lifted his hands out to the side in a show that he meant them no harm. They came on at a gallop, the manes of their horses horizontal. Their yips and screeches filled the clear air in a terrifying show of power.

Ford swallowed hard and felt sweat start to break out on his brow. An awful thought occurred to him. What if he was wrong? What if the Indians rode him down or killed him with their weapons? It appeared that they were about to do just that and he poised to fight. The Nez Perce warriors hauled back on their reins and brought their mounts to a sliding stop.

They stared at him with unfriendly faces while their

mounts stomped and snorted loudly. Ford stared back but waited for them to make the first move.

One of the warriors rode forward and circled him. Ford tensed. The rider stopped in front of Ford and spoke to the deputy marshal in a language Ford could not understand.

'Chuslum Moxmox,' Ford said clearly. He pointed at himself and spoke again, 'Take me to Chuslum Moxmox.'

For a moment, the warrior's face remained passive and Ford thought that his primitive attempt at communication had failed. The man eased his horse forward, pointed at Ford's holstered gun and held out his hand.

Ford nodded his understanding and unbuckled the belt and handed it over. The warrior took it and rode around behind a now unarmed and nervous Ford.

He turned to face the Nez Perce, who pointed off into the distance. Ford nodded his understanding and proceeded in that direction; the long grass stalks whipped around his legs. The warrior watched him go, then followed along behind with his companions.

CHAPTER 13

Hayes looked down at the cold, stiff body of Venters. His eyes were glazed and a bloody hand was at the ugly wound in his throat where he'd tried to plug the hole that allowed his life to bleed out.

The fact that Ford and Brady had managed to get this far was bad in itself. That they'd got their hands on weapons was even worse.

'Over here!' Gibson's shout interrupted the big man's thoughts.

Hayes looked up and saw Gibson waving at him. He walked nearer to the man until he noticed what Gibson had called him over for.

'There, there, there, there, and there.' Gibson pointed them out and Hayes was shocked by the sight before him.

The last one was Lord Bruce's dog, Caesar.

'He don't look so big now, does he?' Hayes said.

'They got Brady but Ford is missin',' Gibson stated.

Hayes nodded. 'Yeah. Spread out. We'll see if we can pick up his trail to find which way he went.'

Ten minutes later, Hayes called Gibson to him.

'He's gone that way.' Hayes pointed to the far ridge. 'Up there.'

Gibson frowned. 'Why that way? Why not follow the trail?'

Hayes shook his head. 'Who knows? Get the horses and we'll track him.'

They followed Ford's vague trail until the afternoon sun began its slow descent and they found the spot where the Nez Perce had come across him.

'That's not good,' Gibson noted.

'Good for us, not for him,' Hayes said.

Gibson smiled coldly. 'They'll peel the hide off him and give him to the squaws to play with. Pity. I was hopin' it would be me who did it for him.'

'Does it matter?'

Gibson shrugged. 'Nope. I guess not.'

'Come on, let's get back,' Hayes said as he pulled his horse around. 'We'll collect the dog and other bodies on our way through.'

Ford guessed there to be approximately an hour's worth of daylight left when they reached the camp on the banks of the Rapid River. He glanced around and estimated somewhere in the vicinity of thirty to forty teepees along it.

The teepees were constructed solidly with a four pole, main framework. Another dozen or so were placed around these to complete the skeleton of the structure. All were lashed firmly into place before the hides were stretched over it and affixed.

Beyond the main camp, a wide meadow contained a large herd of the famed Nez Perce horses. They were certainly a grand sight for a footsore traveller, but a magnificent sight for any horseman.

As they entered the camp, a large crowd gathered to gaze over the stranger in their midst.

They came to a halt near the centre of the encampment in front of a hand-decorated teepee. The elaborate decorations indicated that this was the lodge of Chief Yellow Bull.

A bronzed arm swept back the entrance flap and the opening was filled with the man he'd come to see.

Yellow Bull stood erect and stepped forward, but could not hide the look of surprise on his face when he recognized who stood in front of him.

Ford smiled broadly at him and said, 'I need your help.'

Yellow Bull's face remained passive as he said, 'It would seem spirits look upon you favourably, Josh Ford.'

'Once you hear what I have to say, you might not think so,' Ford replied grimly.

'You are alive,' Yellow Bull pointed out. 'I say that is favourable.'

Ford caught sight of an elk haunch being cooked over a small fire and the smell of roasting meat reached his nostrils. His stomach let out a low growl.

'That sure smells mighty good,' he declared.

Yellow Bull nodded. 'Come inside, Josh Ford. You are welcome in my lodge. While you eat, you tell what help is needed.'

*

Ford wolfed down the meat handed to him by Yellow Bull's wife, Sweet Water. It tasted so good that he asked for more.

'What help you need, Josh Ford?' Yellow Bull asked him.

'I need the help of you and your braves to go back into the valley—'

'No!' Yellow Bull snapped.

'If you'll just let—'

'I say no,' Yellow Bull cut him off again. 'Spirits angry with anyone who enters. And a great beast guards valley, too.'

'The beast is dead,' Ford explained to him. 'I killed it.'

'I doubt very much—'

It was Ford's turn to cut him off. 'The beast was no more than a dog. A very big, ugly dog.' The chief remained silent.

'Just listen to me, to what I have to say,' Ford begged. 'I'll explain it all and you can make up your own mind about whether you want to help or not.'

Yellow Bull nodded. 'Fine. I will listen.'

'Thank you.'

'And I say no.'

For the next twenty minutes, Ford related his story in detail to the Nez Perce chief. His explanations were met with no more than a few grunts until he'd finished.

'So you see,' Ford said in conclusion, 'there are no bad spirits in the valley. The rumblings are just the blasts and the beast was a large dog which is now dead. But I still need your help to rescue those who are being held against their will. It needs to be stopped.'

Yellow Bull contemplated what Ford had told him and said, 'I discuss with others before I answer.'

Ford nodded. 'I understand, but please don't take too long.'

Two hours later, after the disappearance of the sun and much vocal deliberation, Ford was called over to a large fire where five men were seated.

Yellow Bull wore a grave expression on his face. The flickering orange glow from the fire gave it a surreal presence. 'They urge me give no help, send you away, Josh Ford,' the chief explained. Ford looked at the other Indians around the fire. All stared unpleasantly at him. 'But,' Yellow Bull continued, 'I decide, against better judgement and wishes of others, I help free those at mercy of bad man.'

'Thank you,' Ford said, relief visible on his face.

'If this is trap, I kill you myself, Josh Ford.'

Ferguson was incredibly worried. It had never taken this long to recapture an escapee before. Especially when the search party had Caesar with them.

It was long after dark on the following day and there was still no sign of the hunting party or of Hayes and Gibson.

The self-proclaimed Lord sat in his high-backed chair beside the fire. He toyed with a glass of fine brandy, concern etched deeply on his face.

Damn it, where were they? In hindsight, he should have had Ford killed instead of having him flogged. If they managed to bring him back alive, that's what he'd do. Him and the one who'd escaped with him.

The door opened and Hayes entered. Ferguson stood but the look on the big man's face immediately told him that something was wrong. Something bad. 'Well?' Ferguson demanded.

Hayes hesitated briefly and said, 'They're all dead, Lord Bruce.'

Ferguson looked at the big man, a confused look on his face. 'What do you mean, all dead?'

'Every man who went after them is dead,' Hayes elaborated.

Ferguson digested the news. All of the men, Hayes had said.

'Where's Caesar?' he asked.

Again, another hesitation. 'They shot him, too. He's outside. I'm sorry, Lord Bruce, but he's dead.'

Ferguson doubled over as though he'd been punched in the guts. Caesar had been his family, his best friend. And now he was gone.

As he straightened up again, there was a faint tremble in his voice when he spoke and Hayes couldn't tell whether the cause was sadness or anger.

'Get back out there and find them.'

'One of 'em is dead,' Hayes informed him. 'The only one to escape was Ford. If you can call it escape. I doubt we'll be hearin' from him again.'

'Why?'

'The Nez Perce picked him up,' the big man explained. 'Right about now, I expect he's dyin' real slow.'

Ferguson wished that it was he who inflicted the pain

on Ford but held a small amount of satisfaction in the knowledge that the lawman would suffer for killing his dog.

'I'm going to bury Caesar,' Ferguson said solemnly. 'Where is he?'

'We got him on one of the horses,' Hayes replied.

Ferguson nodded and walked slowly past Hayes. Then he stopped and turned to face him.

'The men responsible for their escape. The ones who were on guard and not vigilant enough?'

'Yes, Lord Bruce?'

'Have them locked up tonight ready for the consequences of their actions tomorrow. I want the men to know that I won't tolerate any more mistakes. Lack of diligence isn't acceptable.' Ferguson paused, then, 'I will carry out the punishment myself.'

Hayes's face gave nothing away as he said, 'I'll see to it.'

Without another word, Ferguson walked from the room and left Hayes there alone.

Outside, Ferguson found a horse tethered to the hitch-rail. The carcase of the big wolfhound was draped over it. Ferguson moved closer and stroked the dead animal's fur on his side then lowered his hand to its head.

The lamp inside the building cast its orange glow through the window and illuminated Ferguson's tear-streaked face.

CHAPTER 14

Morning broke the next day and shrouded the valley of Rapid River in a pale mist. Ford watched as twenty warriors prepared their horses for the day's ride.

Somewhere nearby, a baby wailed loudly, woken rudely by the early morning stirrings of the camp. Entranced by the sight of the warriors' preparation, Ford was totally oblivious to the approach of Yellow Bull.

'This is for you, Josh Ford,' the chief announced.

Ford turned to the chief who held out the hackamore reins of a solid looking, grey-dappled horse. Thrown across its back was a blanket and nothing else.

As much as Ford liked the look of the blue roan, this horse was something else entirely.

He took the reins and smiled. 'Thank you.'

Next, Yellow Bull gave him back the six-gun and holster taken from him the previous day. He buckled it on and adjusted it, then checked the loads to ensure all cylinder chambers were full. He would have given just about anything at this point to have his Peacemaker back.

Lastly, Yellow Bull gave Ford an old .44 calibre Henry rifle. It had an octagonal barrel and tarnished brass side plates. There was also a dent towards the end of its tubular magazine so it wouldn't be able to be fully loaded.

Ford checked the action and it was smooth. Apart from the dent, he figured it had been reasonably well looked after.

'Now we go,' Yellow Bull informed him.

Ford mounted the unfamiliar horse and watched as the Nez Perce chief jumped on his own.

With a chorus of war cries, the war party, complete with one Deputy United States Marshal, rode out.

As the rescuers set out from the Indian encampment on the banks of the Rapid River, the punishment of three guards was about to take place.

Two more A-frame scaffolds had been hastily constructed and the three were affixed and naked from the waist up.

All were silent for the moment, their jaws set firm in expectation of the pain that was about to be inflicted. All had seen punishment meted out so they knew what was to come. None knew how bad it was actually going to be.

Ferguson stepped forward to address the whole assembly of guards. All indentured civilians were still locked away.

'As you all know, these three men are responsible for the escape of two prisoners through their inattention to duty,' Ferguson stated in a voice loud enough for them to hear. His tone allowed no misconceptions about what he wanted. 'In doing so, their actions have resulted in the deaths of four men and. . . .'

Ferguson paused to gather himself then continued.

'Four men and my dog Caesar. These three will be made examples of as a reminder of what I expect of you all and what will happen should any of you transgress.'

The gathered crowd remained silent and watched intently as Ferguson removed his own clothes from the waist up.

An audible murmur rippled through the watchers when he turned his back to them, exposing the myriad of scars that crisscrossed his back.

'Yes. As you all can see for yourselves, I too have tasted the lash and from it, I learned one thing. What does not kill you only makes you stronger.'

Ferguson stepped across to the first of the frames and cast sentence upon the three men.

'I have contemplated the seriousness of your crimes and set punishment accordingly,' he told them. 'I have decided that the severity is such that should deter any chance of a reoccurrence. Therefore, each of you shall be subjected to one hundred lashes. . . .'

A sudden uproar rose from the gathered group of assembled guards. The three men begged frantically for mercy. No one had survived fifty, let alone double that figure.

Hayes stepped forward and lifted his Colt into the air.

He fired two shots then shouted at the outraged men.

'Enough! You all heard what the punishment is to be. Just remember this; they are responsible for the deaths of four of our men. Either one of them could have been you. Be thankful it wasn't.'

When he was finished, Hayes turned to face Ferguson and gave him a look that told the Englishman in no uncertain terms that his segundo approved his decision less than the others did. When it was over, two of the three were dead. By some miracle the other was still alive, though wished he wasn't. When Ferguson stepped back, he was bathed in a sheen of sweat that ran red with blood. He turned to face his men who'd remained stoic throughout. His chest heaved from the massive exertion.

'That is what happens to those who put others in peril by not paying attention to what they are doing!' he shouted between gasps for breath. A weak moan escaped the lips of the limp and bloodied man and the Englishman gave him a withering look. With a determined nod, he stalked across to the nearest guard. He relieved the astonished man of his six-gun, a double-action Colt, and returned to the scaffold where the dying man hung. Without hesitation, he raised the gun and squeezed the trigger. The Colt roared and the man's head lurched sideways. Ferguson tossed the Colt back to its owner nonchalantly and said, 'Punishment over.'

Once Ferguson had disappeared, Gibson moved to stand beside Hayes.

'What the hell was all that?' he asked Hayes. 'He didn't have to do that to them.'

'Gettin' soft, Matt?' Hayes said.

Gibson shook his head. 'Nope. I could have shot them myself if I was asked. But they were one of us.'

'And they messed up, Matt,' Hayes hissed. 'They got what they deserved. And now it might keep other minds on their jobs. Now get them settlers back to work.'

Gibson was about to fire back a retort but thought better of it. Instead, he turned on his heel and stomped off. Hayes watched him go but knew Gibson was right. They were some of their own men. If Ferguson wanted to make an example of them, he could have issued the same punishment he'd given Ford. He had a feeling that the loss of his dog had changed something inside the Englishman and thought he'd best keep an eye on him.

The afternoon brought clouds. Great grey, leaden ones that darkened the day and changed afternoon into something akin to night. Thunder began to roll across the peaks of the Bitterroot range in loud percussive waves. Lightning branched out across the sky and drove towards the ground in stabbing forks. It lit the darkened sky in a dazzling display of might and beauty. When the rain finally arrived, it fell in great sheets that soaked the ground and created rivulets that ran off the ridges. It was only a matter of moments before Ford was soaked through. So too were the Nez Perce warriors but they seemed nonplussed by it. Yellow Bull eased his horse in beside Ford and spoke in a voice loud enough to be heard. 'We reach there before night,' he said. Ford nodded. 'I send scouts ahead when we get closer,' he told the deputy marshal. 'We hide in trees while they check pass. When return, we move.'

Ford shivered as a cold trickle of water ran down his back. 'Because we are outnumbered, we need to utilize the darkness to our benefit. The rain will help us but the lightning could be a hindrance.'

'Do not worry,' Yellow Bull assured him. 'Warriors very good. They get in and out, no one know.' They rode on silently as the rain tumbled down and thunder crashed over their heads. With the constant rain came a bone-chilling cold and Ford tried not to think about warm dry clothes and a large fire to warm himself by. Tearing him from his reverie, Yellow Bull suddenly barked out orders that Ford couldn't understand. Three Nez Perce warriors heeled their mounts forward and disappeared through the trees into the gloom.

'We wait here,' Yellow Bull informed him. 'There is cave to shelter from rain while wait.'

'Sounds good to me,' Ford said as a shiver caused his whole body to tremble. The horses were tethered near a large rock outcrop and he followed the Nez Perce chief amongst them until they found the cave. The cave wasn't very big but was enough to hold them all, though it had a distinct animal scent about it. There seemed to be a vague light, nothing bright but sufficient to see by. It was dry and that was what mattered most to Ford. Although he was wet, he had a chance to start to dry out and warm up a little. One of the braves managed to get a small fire going and the warmth soon radiated around the cave. They'd been there two hours when Yellow Bull sat down beside him and asked, 'Do you have knife?'

'No,' Ford answered.

'I get one before we enter valley.'

Ford noticed an expression of concern on the chief's face.

'What's up? You look worried.'

'After we here I send three warriors to scout.'

109

'Yes. I saw that. But you told me you were going to.'

'One I send to look where you said fight with other men took place,' Yellow Bull explained. 'When he return he tell me what he found. Not that I not trust you, but want be certain.'

Ford understood and said as much. 'I thought you might, just to be sure. They were there? The bodies?'

'Yes,' Yellow Bull said.

'And no.'

'What do you mean?'

'The bodies of men gone,' Yellow Bull told him. 'All but one.'

Ford guessed whose body had been left behind. It had to be Brady. 'And the dog?'

'No, it gone, too.'

'If whoever took the bodies followed my trail, then they'll know that your braves picked me up,' Ford hypothesized.

Yellow Bull grunted his agreement. 'Maybe they think you captive instead of us help you.'

'Let's hope so,' Ford said. 'Because if they don't, then it is goin' to be one hell of a job freein' those prisoners.'

CHAPTER 15

The storm had abated marginally by the time the two Nez Perce warriors returned. They spoke briefly with Yellow Bull then the chief barked a few orders and the others exited the cave.

He turned towards Ford and said, 'We go. Two guards in pass scouts take care of. When get to valley we use knives.'

He passed Ford a knife he'd borrowed from one of his warriors. Ford nodded his thanks and followed the Nez Perce chief out of the cave.

A razor-sharp blade across the throat dispatched the first two guards. A firmly clamped hand over the mouth prevented the escape of any noise which might raise the alarm and alert others of the situation. The noise of the rain and thunder would be sufficient to cover any sounds made.

When they finally exited the pass, the storm had mostly subsided and the rain had almost stopped. The rumble of thunder still echoed in the distance, an indicator of the storm's direction of travel. The occasional flash of lightning illuminated the valley less now that it had moved further away.

Yellow Bull came up beside Ford and said, 'We are ready.'

'I'll start to free the captives while you and your warriors go to work thinnin' 'em out,' Ford told the Nez Perce chief.

'Take one my men with you,' Yellow Bull said. 'He help you.'

Ford wasn't quite certain about the suggestion, but after a moment of consideration, he could see the sense in it. 'OK.'

The warrior that Yellow Bull picked out was tall and solid. Nothing more specific could be detected in the darkness, but he imagined the man's face wore a scowl.

His name . . . Yellow Bull paused for a moment as he thought of a translation for the name so Ford could understand it . . . Lame Elk,' he finished.

'Let's go then,' Ford said as he moved out into the darkness.

A blast of cold damp air shot through the narrow opening and permeated the dark room as the door was slammed back on its hinges. A large figure with a lantern filled the space that the heavy wooden door had just vacated.

The man moved into the room with purpose, his focus specific and determined. He bent over the cowering form of Allison Ellis, grabbed a fistful of blonde hair and hauled her to her feet. 'You're comin' with me,' Gibson rasped, his voice thick with lust. A violent struggle ensued and Allison let out an ear-piercing scream that brought everyone in the immediate vicinity awake with a start. She continued to kick and slap with all her might and struck out at him with clawed fingers and raked Gibsons's face. He responded with vicious intent, an open palm caught her heavily across the cheek with a resounding crack. Instantly, she went weak at the knees and her struggles ceased. 'Give me any more trouble and I'll cut your throat,' Gibson warned Allison as he dragged her out of the door and into the rain. The slam of the door rattled the building to its foundations.

From the shadows, Ford watched Lame Elk loom up silently behind a guard and draw the blade across his throat. The man had been oblivious to the impending danger and paid for his complacency. His body twitched spasmodically as he was dragged and lowered into the shadows of the brush.

Ford joined the brave and knelt to strip the corpse of armaments he would no longer require. He relieved him of a rifle and his six-gun. They moved forward stealthily, prepared to take down any opposition they might run into. The small log prison that was Ford's target came into view and they moved quietly alongside the rough-hewn building. He looked about quickly then stepped up to the door to slip the latch when a guard appeared from the other side of the structure. 'What the hell?' he gasped.

The man raised the rifle he held and drew in a deep breath to raise the alarm. The only sound Ford heard was a dull thunk and a knife handle sprouted from the guard's chest. The man collapsed without further sound.

Lame Elk quietly moved forward and bent down to

retrieve his knife from the dead man's chest. He wiped the blood from the blade on the clothes of his latest victim.

'Thanks,' Ford whispered, grateful now that the Nez Perce warrior was along. Lame Elk responded with a grunt. Ford opened the latch and swung the door open. 'Finn,' he called softly. 'Finn, are you here?'

'Is that you, Ford?' he asked, a hint of exasperation in his rough voice. 'What in hell are you doin' back here?'

'We came to get you all out,' Ford explained.

'We? Is Brady with you?'

'Brady's dead,' he said bluntly. 'I'll give you the details later. Right now we need to get to the rest of the prisoners and turn them loose. Some can help the women and children, but we still need a few of the more capable men to help take down the guards.'

'Holy Hanna,' one of the other prisoners gasped. 'It's an Indian.'

Lame Elk stood in the doorway and a distant flash of lightning lit him perfectly for all to see.

'Easy,' Ford warned. 'The Nez Perce are here to help.'

'I guess Yellow Bull listened to you, huh? Man, to think I had my doubts.'

'Come on, we have to move,' Ford said. 'Finn, can you get them all organized?'

'Sure.'

'Just remember, no noise.'

'No problem,' Finn assured him.

Two minutes later, a single gunshot sent everything to hell.

Out beyond the horse corral, out of earshot from the

114

rest of the camp, Gibson pushed Allison Ellis roughly along in front of him towards a stand of larch. She sobbed quietly and stumbled along the rough path.

A guard caught them unawares when he appeared in front of the pair. 'Help me, please,' Allison pleaded desperately.

'What are you doin' out here, Gibson? Didn't Hayes tell you to leave that girl alone?' the guard asked.

'How about you shut up and mind your own damned business,' Gibson snarled back.

'Hey, your hide, not mine. You do what you want with it.'

'And just you remember that,' Gibson hissed at the man then pushed Allison so hard in the back that she tumbled to the ground. He reefed her up by the arm and forced her onward. They'd gone not more than ten paces when a large figure loomed out of the darkness in front of them. A flash of lightning illuminated the face of a warrior, knife raised above his head. Allison's shrill scream split the night, terrified at the unexpected and frightful sight facing them. Gibson froze momentarily then instinct took over. The blackness had enveloped them again after the lightning flash, but he drew his Colt and fired in the direction he'd last seen the Indian.

The six-gun roared and a grunt from in front of them told him that his aim was sure as the warrior took the slug in his chest. The next flash of lightning shed light upon the warrior's body in the mud at their feet.

'Indians in the camp!' Gibson shouted loudly. 'There's damned Indians in the camp! Get up!' The guard he'd spoken to previously appeared beside him.

'What in hell is goin' on?'

'There's Indians in the camp. Get everybody up.'

The man ran off and Gibson grabbed Allison roughly by the arm. She trembled with fear from the confrontation and now cried out at the sudden pain of his harsh grip. He bent to drag her back towards the small log-built prison.

They got as far as the horse corral when the whole camp erupted with shouts, war cries, gunshots and the screams of dying men.

The guard who'd gone off to warn the others came back towards them at a run. 'They're everywhere!' he exclaimed, his voice filled with panic. 'They're killin' everyone.'

'Damn it,' Gibson cursed. 'Get three horses saddled while I keep an eye out.' The guard jumped into the pole corral while Gibson pushed Allison aside and sat her down. 'If you don't want to die, stay right there,' he ordered her. 'I'm goin' to help with the horses. Just pray some buck don't find you before we're finished.'

Hayes burst into the room and found Ferguson standing there with a cocked Remington in his fist. The self-proclaimed Lord swung it towards Hayes as he entered. 'Whoa!' Hayes cried out. 'Don't shoot, it's just me.'

'What on earth is going on, Mr Hayes?' Ferguson demanded.

'Indians,' Hayes blurted out, panic in his eyes. 'The whole camp has been overrun by Indians. They're killin' everyone they come across. We're losin' men everywhere, it's a slaughter. If we stay we'll die.'

Ferguson knew that the situation was dire. He'd never witnessed panic in Hayes in all the years he'd known him. The big man was generally a picture of calm. 'What do you propose then, man?' Ferguson asked.

'We need to get some horses and light out of here,' Hayes said hurriedly.

'But what about the gold? The men?'

'To hell with it all,' Hayes half yelled. 'If we don't leave now, we'll be as dead as the rest of them. We can always come back later for the gold.'

Ferguson nodded. 'Let's go.'

CHAPTER 16

Ford and Lame Elk made their way stealthily along to the next log-built prison to release more captives when all hell broke loose.

'Hell,' he muttered. 'That's torn it.' The night erupted in orange flashes as gunfire rang out. Shouts of panic and war cries that would make a snake's blood run cold echoed around the secluded valley.

Ford dropped the knife, brought up the Henry rifle and eared back the hammer.

'Finn,' he called back to the old man. 'Don't let any more out.' Finn ran across to him. 'Why?'

'It'll be safer if they stay locked away behind thick walls with bullets flying around. For the time being anyway,' Ford explained. 'Find yourselves some weapons and let's get to it. And don't no one shoot any Indians.' To the right of Finn, a figure lumbered out of the dark with a rifle in his hands. Ford swung the Henry up and fired. The bullet ploughed into the man's middle and stopped him cold. Ford levered another round into the Henry's breech and fired again. This time, the .44 calibre slug punched into his chest and knocked him onto his back. 'Damn,' Finn gasped out.

'Get movin',' Ford snapped. 'I'm goin' after that son of a bitch Ferguson.' Ford hurried off with Lame Elk behind him.

Distant lightning brightened the sky once more and revealed a man staggering drunkenly from the brush directly into the path of Ford and the Indian, who noticed a knife buried hilt deep in his chest. Ford kept on. As he drew level with the wounded guard, he slammed his rifle butt into the side of the man's head. The outlaw fell as though pole-axed and moved no more.

Upon arrival at Ferguson's home, they found the door wide open, the room lit with dull lamp light. Ford and Lame Elk entered cautiously, the deputy marshal ready with his finger on the rifle's trigger.

They checked the room to make sure that Ferguson hadn't hidden himself away but found it empty. Ford picked up a kerosene lamp and moved over to a small table.

The sound of heavy boots on the timber veranda outside announced the arrival of a man who burst through the entry with a Colt in his fist.

He stopped abruptly, surprise etched on his face. The momentary lapse provided the time that Lame Elk needed.

The Nez Perce warrior reached for his tomahawk and with a fluid snap of his wrist, released the deadly weapon. Its charge spun through the air and buried itself in the man's chest. He dropped to the floor like a stone and Lame Elk hurried forward to retrieve his weapon. Ford nodded, impressed by the speed and efficiency of the dispatch. He turned his attention back to the lamp in his hand, looked about thoughtfully, then threw it at the far wall. It shattered on impact and sprayed kerosene across the surface of the wall and surrounding furniture which burst instantly into flames. Large orange tongues flicked out greedily and began to consume everything soaked by the pungent fuel.

'Come on,' Ford said to Lame Elk. 'Let's get out of here.'

Once outside, away from the crackle of the fire, Ford could hear that the previous cacophony of gunfire had dwindled to sporadic pops.

They stepped down off the veranda and Ford sensed a movement to his right and brought the Henry around ready to fire.

'It's me, don't shoot,' Finn called to him.

Ford took his finger from the trigger and said, 'Get yourself shot sneakin' up on a man like that. Come on over.' Finn moved closer and stopped in front of Ford.

'We got 'em licked,' he chortled. 'By golly we have. Them Indians are moppin' the rest of 'em up now.'

Ford breathed a sigh of relief. 'Good. We can start lettin' the rest of the prisoners out.'

'Did you get Ferguson?'

'No, he wasn't there.'

'Well, maybe the Indians got him,' the old timer suggested.

'Maybe,' Ford said. 'But I ain't seen hide nor hair of Hayes and Gibson, either.'

'Now you mention it, me neither.'

'I guess we'll have to wait until sun up to find out then.'

*

In the light of day, the carnage of the previous night was evident for all to see. The Nez Perce had shown no mercy. The bodies of the outlaws lay strewn everywhere. Freed settlers walked around in a daze and the once solid home of Lord Bruce Ferguson was now a smouldering ruin.

A silent wraith appeared at Ford's side as he surveyed the grisly sight.

'Did you find men you seek, Josh Ford?' Yellow Bull asked.

Ford shook his head. 'They are not here. How many warriors did you lose?'

'Three,' he replied. 'But your people are free. This what we came here for.'

Ford nodded. He wasn't happy about Ferguson's escape, or the loss of Yellow Bull's warriors, but the liberation of the prisoners eased that hurt some.

He watched as Finn hurried towards him, a look of concern etched on his face.

'For a free man you look awful worried,' Ford ventured as the man stopped in front of him.

'That's 'cause we got a problem,' he declared.

Ford's face hardened. 'What problem?'

'Right before all hell broke loose last night, that son of a bitch Gibson took the Ellis girl,' Finn blustered. 'They ain't nowhere in this damn camp.'

'Hell,' Ford snarled, 'I'm goin' to have to run him to ground before he hurts her. Where did they store the guns and such they took from the settlers? I want my own weapons back.'

'I can't be certain, but I have an idea. Come with me,'

121

Finn urged him. Ford and Yellow Bull hurried after the man.

The three of them found what they needed in a dug out cellar with a log roof.

'There's enough. . . .' started Finn but his voice trailed away.

'Yeah,' Ford agreed. Rows of rifles, handguns, and boxes of ammunition and dynamite lined the walls. After a quick scout around, Ford found his Colt Peacemaker and his Winchester rifle.He buckled on the six-gun and tied down the holster with the rawhide thong.

'Right,' Ford said, satisfied. 'Now all I need is somethin' to ride.'

'There he is,' Ford said as he pointed out the blue roan on the far side of the corral.

The deputy marshal gave a piercing whistle and the horse lifted his head and swung around. It looked at Ford and started in his direction. Ford adjusted the saddle in his arms and walked out to meet him.He saddled the roan and mounted him quickly, then turned to face Yellow Bull and Finn.

'You want me come with you?' Yellow Bull asked him.

'No,' Ford said with a shake of his head. 'This is somethin' I want to do by myself. Can you and your people stay here to keep an eye on things until I return?'

The big chief nodded.

'I do this,' he told Ford.

'Finn, where is that back way out you mentioned?' Ford asked.

'I heard it was to the north,' Finn answered uncertainly. 'There's meant to be a notch thereabouts.'

'I'll find it if it's there,' Ford assured him and kneed the roan forward.

The notch was easy enough to find, the churned earth at the turnoff from the recent activity acted like a directional beacon so he knew that he was on the right track.

The trail became rocky and wound its way to the notch halfway up the ridge line. It was instantly obvious why pack trains were the largest things able to traverse the dangerous route.

He let the roan pick his way up the slope at a slow speed. When it topped out, the trail passed through a narrow crevice with a hard-packed base.

The far end opened out onto a lush, green bench that looked out over a broad valley. He looked down and saw a large meadow full of wildflowers; a cascade of yellows, purples, and pinks contrasted against their light green backdrop.

Cottonwood trees lined a winding stream and large stands of spruce reached towards the clear blue sky. Ford followed the trail down from the bench. It passed between large rocky outcrops before it flattened out on the valley floor. The trail he was on suddenly split and went in two separate directions. The churned up earth indicated that two horses had turned left while three had gone right. Five riders. Ford guessed the pair to be Ferguson and Hayes while another two would be the girl and Gibson. He tried to consider who the third rider might be and who was he most likely to travel with. Ford eased the roan to a halt and studied both trails. The two horses may well be Gibson and the girl, but, as the trail led to the east, it was a more likely route for Ferguson and Hayes to have taken. He pointed the roan at the right-hand fork and began to follow that. He decided to rescue the girl first then go after Ferguson. Besides, he had an idea where they were headed anyway.

The sun sat high in a cloud-streaked sky. Overhead, an eagle circled in search of prey.

Three horses followed an overgrown trail lined with waist high grass. The rider named Carlin called out for Gibson to stop. 'What's wrong?' Gibson asked as he turned his mount so he could see the man.

The outlaw had dismounted and now examined his horse's off-side front hoof.

He looked up at Gibson and shook his head. 'Damn thing has gone lame on me. He ain't goin' no further.'

'Well, we ain't stoppin',' Gibson informed him.

'That's fine,' Carlin said, 'I'll just climb on up behind the girl and ride double.'

Gibson shook his head. 'Nope. You ain't ridin' double with her. You walk.'

'You're kiddin', ain't you?' Carlin said incredulously. 'I'm climbin' up behind the girl and that's all there is to it.'

He approached the horse that Allison sat atop.

Gibson drew his six-gun and eared back the hammer. 'Does this look like I'm kiddin'?'

Carlin froze. 'What? Are you goin' to shoot me for wantin' to ride double with the girl?'

'I will if you go anywhere near that horse,' Gibson said coldly.

Carlin's shoulders sagged like a beaten man and he nodded his acceptance.

'I knew you'd see it my way,' Gibson said with a smile.

'Yeah, I do.'

Gibson holstered his gun and turned his back on the guard. As he did, Carlin's hand dived for his six-gun. The almost inaudible intake of breath by Allison was all the warning Gibson received of his impending fate. He threw himself sideways from the saddle as the gun in Carlin's fist thundered. The bullet passed through empty space and flew harmlessly away. His shoulder slammed into the hard ground and the whole of his body was jarred mercilessly from the impact. He rolled and ignored the shooting pain that coursed through his body and came up on one knee, Colt in hand. He fired two quick shots, the first of which passed harmlessly over Carlin's left shoulder. The second, however, found its target. It penetrated the outlaw's chest and punched through his lung. Carlin went down heavily on his back, his six-gun spilled from his grip.

He lay there, stunned at the speed of the exchange, his mouth worked as he tried to suck in air, only to have most of it escape from the ragged wound in his chest. Gibson stood up and worked a rotation into his injured shoulder as he walked across to where Carlin lay. He looked down at the slowly dying man and shook his head.

'Never would have figured you for a backshooter, Carlin,' he surmised. 'Just goes to show how a man can be wrong.'

Without a further word, Gibson thumbed back the hammer and shot Carlin one more time.

CHAPTER 17

Ford drew back on the reins of the roan as the faint echo of gunfire rolled from further along the valley.

He gave voice to his immediate concerns. 'That don't sound too good, horse.'

He dropped his hand to the Peacemaker and left it to rest there as he eased the horse forward. His body rocked fluidly with the roan's movements as it picked its way along the thread of a trail. It appeared that he had gained some ground on those ahead of him as the hoof-churned earth out front was still damp. He hoped to close the distance before dark to gain an edge.

Ford found Carlin's body soon after, left where he had been shot mercilessly by Gibson. The outlaw's horse cropped grass off to the side of the trail, its injured hoof obviously favoured.

'Looks like somebody had a fallin' out,' he muttered. 'At least we know who the third rider was. It would appear that he ain't goin' to be a problem no more.'

A brief thought about a decent burial for the man

crossed his mind but he dismissed it just as quick. After their actions towards the settlers, he and his cohorts sure as hell didn't deserve to be treated with respect. Instead, Ford unsaddled the injured horse to allow him to roam free then continued to follow the trail of Gibson and Allison Ellis.

'This'll do,' Gibson said. 'Get off your horse. We'll camp here.'

The spot that Gibson had chosen for his night camp was at the edge of a stand of spruce trees. It was sheltered and offered fresh water by way of a small stream with a pebble bottom. Allison almost fell from the saddle. Bone tired and sore from the ride and her earlier rough treatment, she staggered a little before she found herself the trunk of a deadfall to seat herself on.

'What do you think you're doin?' Gibson snapped.

She looked at him open-mouthed. 'Get some wood so we can get a fire goin',' he ordered her. With a groan, Allison climbed wearily to her feet and began to look about for dry sticks and branches for the fire.

'And don't think about tryin' to run off. I'd shoot you before you got five steps.'

Gibson hobbled the horses then stood and watched as she went about her work as ordered.

Allison looked around and caught him in an obvious leer and she stood up. 'When are we going to arrive at a town?'

Gibson snorted. 'We ain't goin' to no town. Just 'cause I got you away from them Indians don't mean I'm goin' to let you go. I ain't stupid, you know. Besides, I got plans for you.'

Her blood ran cold at the lustful look he gave her and she shivered at the thought of what this evil man dressed in putrid buckskins might do to her.

Allison went back to her firewood collection and before long, brought a small pile to the circle of rocks Gibson had set up.

She eyed him cautiously as he lit the fire, and simultaneously assessed her chances of escape into the surrounding forest. They were slim at best as he was too vigilant and never took his eyes from her for more than a few seconds.

As Allison looked around, the cold realization of how alone and defenceless she was struck her like a physical blow and she gasped. Her father was gone and there was no one to rescue her. Way out here, nobody would hear her screams.

Ford could see the orange glow of a campfire in the distance. The night was cool and dark and the flickering light stood out like a beacon as he approached. He guessed that it had to be his quarry.

The blue roan had been pressed hard throughout the day without let up; the thought of what Gibson might do to the girl had spurred Ford on. The horse had endured the long ride well and reminded him why, despite all of its ornery behaviours, he would never willingly part with the animal. 'Looks like we found 'em, boy,' Ford said softly. He slowed the horse to a walk. When he judged them to be close enough, he eased the animal off the trail and into the trees. He brought the horse to a stop when he figured they were a safe distance away. He dismounted and looped the reins over the saddle horn. The roan would stay put, but in case the horse had to take flight suddenly, it could be dangerous to have them dangling, which increased the risk of snag and injury. 'I'll be back. Don't go anywhere.' Ford drew his Peacemaker and started forward. He headed for the glow that was visible in the distance, which guided him through the trees towards the camp. As he got closer, he could hear two voices, one male, and the other female. There was movement beyond the flickering firelight, then a woman's scream pierced the night.

Gibson came at her in a rush. Allison circled the fire in a vain attempt to evade his advances. He'd made his intentions clear to her in the preceding few moments and had chosen this instant to act on them. She cried streams of tears in fear as she considered running out into the dark night.

Without warning, Gibson leapt across the flames and grabbed her in a bear hug before she could escape. He forced his face close to hers and she screamed just before his lips crushed hers in a brutal kiss. Allison gagged with disgust as his body odour and foul breath assailed her nostrils. She clawed at his face and her nails opened up furrows in his left cheek, in addition to the scabbed over ones he already sported. He laughed loudly, a maniacal sound that sent shivers down her spine. Gibson shoved Allison roughly to the ground and stood over her.

'Hold it, Gibson.' Ford's voice cracked like a whip

from beyond the firelight. The outlaw dropped his hand to his gun and whirled about in time to see Ford emerge from the darkness, a cocked six-gun in his fist. 'Pull it and I'll kill you,' Ford warned him.

'What the hell are you still doin' alive?' Gibson asked, shocked. 'I was sure them Indians had done for you.'

'Not hardly,' Ford answered and then dropped his eyes to Allison. 'Get up, ma'am, and move away from him.'

Stunned by the sudden appearance of the familiar face, Allison scrambled to her feet and backed away from the imminent confrontation. She sniffed and wiped her tears as she went. Ford's gaze went back to Gibson. 'I see you left a body on your back trail. Death seems to follow you around, don't it?'

'So what now?' enquired Gibson. 'Are you goin' to slap some irons on me and take me in?'

Ford slipped his Peacemaker back into its holster, his grim smile visible in the orange glow. 'Nope.'

Gibson returned Ford's smile with a cold one of his own. 'I been itchin' to do this for a good while now.'

'Then have at it.'

Gibson's shoulder dipped and his hand locked onto the walnut grips of his Colt. He began to draw the gun from its holster then froze as he stared down the barrel of Ford's Peacemaker. Gibson grimaced at the realization that he was about to die. He had been outclassed and could do nothing to stop it. He let out a snarl and continued to pull his weapon. It had just cleared leather when Ford's Colt roared. The .45 calibre slug punched into Gibson's chest and he staggered with the impact.

130

Reflexively, he squeezed the trigger but the slug ploughed harmlessly into the earth. In a desperate effort, the outlaw tried to raise his six-gun higher and bring it into line. The weight of the gun was immense as his strength quickly ebbed out of him and he fell face forward to the ground. As the echoes of the shots died away, Ford remained poised for action if Gibson moved. When he didn't, Ford stepped closer to the dead man and nudged him with the toe of his boot. 'Is . . . is he dead?' Allison asked.

'As dead as he's ever goin' to be,' Ford confirmed.

'Oh thank God,' said Allison, relief evident in her voice. 'I thought he was going to . . . was going . . . was. . . .'

She couldn't formulate the words and clapped her hands to her face in an effort to block out the image of what had almost been. Ford watched her shoulders begin to tremble uncontrollably as the relief at her narrow escape hit her. He walked over to her and asked, 'Are you OK , ma'am?' Allison looked at him through tear filled eyes then burst into loud sobs as she fell into his arms.

On their return to the valley late the following day, they found most of the Nez Perce warriors had gone. A small handful remained behind, Yellow Bull included.

Finn came up to Ford and said, 'I see you got the girl back.'

'Yeah,' Ford said as he watched as she was led away.

'What about Gibson?' Finn asked.

'He won't be botherin' anyone no more,' Ford explained. 'How are they all holdin' up?'

'They're all mighty eager to be shuck of this place,' Finn told him.

Ford nodded. 'Yeah. Can't blame 'em for that. They'll just have to wait a little longer.'

'But why?' the old timer said, confused.

'I'm goin' to head out to Fort Williamson after my horse has rested up overnight,' Ford informed him. 'I'll get 'em to send out a detail with a doctor and such to check everybody over.' He cast a glance at Yellow Bull. 'Is that OK with you?'

The big Nez Perce chief nodded. 'It is fine.'

'So you'll be comin' back with 'em, right?' Finn said.

Ford shook his head. 'No, I'm goin' after Hayes and Ferguson.'

'But they'll be miles away by now,' Finn protested.

'I have a feelin' about where they're headin',' Ford said.

'Seattle?'

'That's where I'm headed,' he confirmed.

'Good luck with that then,' Finn said sceptically.

As the early sunlight left fingers of a red-orange hue across the valley the next day, Ford rode out of the valley through the tree-choked pass. Beside him rode Yellow Bull and his few remaining warriors.

When they reached the main trail, Ford turned his roan to face the Nez Perce chief. 'Thank you for all of your help, Chuslum Moxmox,' he said, using the chief's Nez Perce name out of respect. Yellow Bull smiled. It was the first time that Ford could remember him doing so.

'I hope you count Nez Perce as friend, Josh Ford,

because we count you as one,' he said as he moved his own mount forward and extended his hand. Ford took it and returned the smile. 'I am honoured to count the Nez Perce, my friend.'

'That is good.'

'Could you do somethin' else for me?' Ford asked hesitantly.

'Ask and will see.'

'The man that was left behind, Brady, could you. . . ?'

'He was friend?' Yellow Bull said.

'Yes.'

'I take care of it myself,' Yellow Bull confirmed.

'Thank you, my friend,' Ford said.

'Here, may need this,' the Nez Perce chief said and held out the knife that he'd originally given Ford.

Ford took it and nodded.

'Be careful, Josh Ford,' Yellow Bull warned. 'A snake in grass is not easily seen.'

CHAPTER 18

Fort Williamson was situated at the junction of two clear-water streams in the Elk Horn valley. It was surrounded by high tree-lined hills and beyond them were high, craggy peaks.

The fort was not fortified by stockade walls as many were. Instead, it was merely a handful of scattered buildings around a central parade ground.

Ford sat on a hard wooden chair in the commander's office and had just finishing relating his story to the man.

'That sure is some story, Marshal Ford,' Colonel Brad Weston said to Ford.

'They're goin' to need your help, Colonel,' Ford urged. 'They've all been in a bad way for a long time.'

Yes, quite,' Weston agreed on reflection. 'I'll dispatch a troop and the post surgeon as soon as possible.'

'You won't have trouble with the Nez Perce,' Ford said. 'If it hadn't been for them, none of this would have been possible.'

Weston stood up from his chair and walked across to a dust-streaked window and looked out at the activity on the parade ground, hands behind his back.

134

'It makes me wonder, Ford, how things like this can happen,' Weston said, still trying to get his head around it. 'And this man is an English Lord, you say?'

'He's no more a Lord than I am,' snorted Ford derisively. 'He's English, sure, but from what I can figure, he's a sailor. My guess is he's a navy man who deserted his ship when it hit port up in Canada and never looked back. As for the part about bringing the dog with him, well, he could have picked it up as a pup from anywhere. Maybe even some immigrants.'

'But how do you know he's from a ship?' Weston asked.

'He called the whip he was usin' the Captain's Daughter,' Ford explained. 'Only a sailor would use that term.'

'So what will you do now?' Weston enquired. 'Where do you begin to search for them?'

'He was shippin' his ore by mule to Seattle,' Ford answered. 'I'm thinkin' he'll head there. Try and get himself and the gold on a ship. Apparently there is someone else workin' that end.'

'It would have to be somebody he trusts a lot,' Weston pointed out.

'I guess I'll find out when I get there. Providin' that's where they are.'

Weston nodded. 'Is there anything else I can do for you?'

'Where's the nearest telegraph hereabouts?'

'A little town about forty miles north of here called Parkin,' Weston informed him.

'No good, it's in the wrong direction.'

'How about you write down what you want to say and I'll send a rider there and he'll send it for you?' Weston suggested. 'If that will help you any?'

Ford thought about the offer. It would save him time. 'OK.'

'I'll just get you a pencil and paper,' Weston told him. 'If I send the rider now, he should arrive there some time tonight.'

'Thanks, Colonel, I sure appreciate it.'

Bass Reeves tried to concentrate on his work but no word from or about Josh was starting to play on his mind. So much so that he contemplated the addition of five of his best men to the case. He could send them into the Bitterroots to find out what had happened.

Bismarck began to stir soon after dawn broke and its residents went about their business along the streets. The noise level rose gradually as the morning progressed.

The city, originally called Edwinton, was founded when the Northern Pacific Railroad reached the banks of the Missouri in 1872. A year later, the name was changed to Bismarck and the city became the county seat for Burleigh County. Bismarck was growing steadily. Its population of permanent residents had just hit 1,700 citizens, not including drifters and outlaws. One of those citizens walked through the door to the marshal's office and interrupted Reeves' non-productive start to the morning. Reeves looked up from behind his dark timber desk. 'What can I do for you at this time of the mornin', Bart?'

Bart, the local telegraphist, was a thinly built man who

wore glasses and a perpetual frown upon his face. He waved a piece of paper in the air and said, 'This came in last night. It's for you. It came from Parkin, Montana.'

It was Reeves's turn to frown and he held out his hand to take the paper. Bart passed it over and as he turned to leave, Reeves' voice stopped him.

'Just hold up a minute in case I need to reply.'

Bart shrugged and walked over to a wooden chair in the corner and sat down.

Reeves finished the message, frowned and read it again.

He looked up at Bart. 'I'll write you two messages and I want them sent as soon as possible. One is for the Governor of Montana and the other is for Deputy United States Marshal Archie Wyatt in Seattle.'

Ford stopped the roan on a rise and looked out across the city of Seattle to the harbour.

Seattle was a burgeoning town; its population had grown from a mere 188 people in 1860 to a point now where it was home to just over 3,500. It was a town on the rise. Somewhere down there were the men he sought, he was certain of it. He hoped that the deputy marshal based in Seattle had been successful in his search for something that might help lead him to the men. He kneed the roan forward. 'Come on, horse, let's go and find out what he knows.'

Ford took in his surroundings as he rode along Front Street. The dirt street sloped away from him and on his right was a hardware store. To his left, a shop sign advertised boots and shoes and further on, another had a sign for a beer hall.

He continued on until he found the marshal's office. Ford tethered the roan outside then climbed up onto the uneven boardwalk. Two men dressed impeccably in black frock coats and top hats watched him closely as he did so.

Ford realized that he must look a sight. He was dirty and unshaven but he couldn't have cared less. He had one reason only for this visit: to arrest Hayes and Ferguson. If they were indeed in Seattle. Hinges squeaked their protest as he pushed the door open and entered the spartan office. A man seated behind a heavily marked desk looked up to see who it was.

Ford closed the door behind him and crossed the short distance to where the man was seated.

'I'm Josh Ford,' Ford announced. 'I believe you are expectin' me?'

The look of recognition on the man's face suggested that he was. The man stood up and thrust out a calloused hand. 'Yes. I'm Archie Wyatt. Bass sent word you were comin' and asked that I help you in any way I can. Welcome to Seattle.'

United States Deputy Marshal Archie Wyatt was a thinly built man who Ford guessed to be early to mid-forties from the amount of grey in his black hair. 'What else did Bass say?' Ford asked sceptically.

'Just to help you in any way possible and he told me who you were chasin',' Wyatt explained. 'I had me a look around Seattle to see what I could come up with for you.'

'And?'

'Not one to delay, are you?' Wyatt observed.

'Don't have time,' Ford said abruptly.

Wyatt sat back down in his chair and pointed at another at the edge of his desk. 'Take a seat.'

'I'll stand,' Ford said. 'Tell me what you found.'

'Not what. Who.'

Ford frowned. 'You've found them?'

'Not exactly,' Wyatt said. 'I asked around about the obvious because I thought an Englishman would stand out. What I found out was that a few years back, a lumber man who had an operation in the hills outside of Seattle, rented a large shed to an Englishman.'

'Had?'

'Yeah, he died not long after and his operation shut down.'

'I see.'

'But it don't end there,' Wyatt assured him. 'That buildin' is still there and it is still bein' used by the same person.'

'At least that's somethin',' Ford said. 'Do you think it could be Ferguson?'

'If it is, that ain't the name he's usin',' Wyatt told him. 'And therein lies the problem.'

Ford frowned. 'What problem?'

'The gent you claim might be this Ferguson feller is actually Emerson Peacock. He's the richest businessman in Seattle.'

'So?'

'If you want my advice you'll leave this one alone, Ford,' Wyatt warned. 'He knows more senators and governors than any man I know of. Hell, he's even got judges in his pocket. He spends a lot of his time back east. And. . . .'

139

'And I bet he's just come from back east on some trip, hasn't he?'

'So the story goes,' Wyatt confirmed.

'Did he come here with his fortune or was it acquired after his arrival?' Ford snapped. 'I'll tell you, he got rich on the blood of others.'

Wyatt shrugged. 'Does it matter? The point is, you can't do anythin' about this feller, Ford. Just go back to where you came from and forget it. Tell head office that they escaped.'

Ford shook his head as he thought about the suffering caused by the man and his cohorts. 'Nope. Can't do it. Let's go check out this buildin' you were tellin' me about. If he's keepin' his ore somewhere, then that'll be it.'

'OK. But don't say that I didn't warn you,' Wyatt said resignedly.

CHAPTER 19

The mill sat a mile outside Seattle in a patch of densely forested hills. Large cedars reached up into the sky, their tops disappeared into a low sea mist which had blown in.

, A shiver went down Ford's spine, but he couldn't be certain whether it was from the mist or something else. The words of Yellow Bull filled his head. 'A snake in the grass is not easily seen.' For a disused lumber mill, all of the plank-built buildings and equipment looked to be in good repair. Ford thought that the buildings should show some sign of neglect and decay. Both men stopped their horses on a large bare patch of earth outside a large shed. They sat for a short while as Ford surveyed the eerie scene. It seemed to be a ghost town. 'If Ferguson, as you know him, keeps his ore and such here, where would he smelt the gold?' Wyatt pondered.

'You say that he's the richest man in Seattle, right?'

'That's right,' Wyatt confirmed.

'Does he own any boats, ships, I mean?'

'A couple,' he answered. 'They run freight for him up and down the coast. That is part of his business.'

'So he doesn't need to smelt it here. He could just load it onto one of his ships and take it wherever.'

'I guess he could do that,' Wyatt agreed.

'Well, let's find out what he keeps here,' Ford said, climbing down from the roan's back. They walked over to the door which Ford opened. The inside was dim, lit only by the light from outside which filtered through cracks in the plank walls. Ford was about to step inside when the triple-click of a gun hammer and barrel against his spine, made him freeze.

'Get your hands up and move inside,' Wyatt ordered. 'And no sudden moves or I'll put a slug in your back.'

Ford raised his hands to shoulder level and slowly walked through the open doorway. The building contained sacks of ore from the mine in the Bitterroots. Once far enough inside Wyatt snapped, 'That'll do. Now, turn around.'

Ford turned to face the traitor. Wyatt licked his lips nervously and his gun hand trembled slightly.

'Unbuckle the gun belt and let it drop.'

Ford did as he was ordered.

'Now step back.'

With Ford disarmed and away from him, tension in the deputy marshal eased slightly.

'I guess Yellow Bull was right,' Ford muttered.

'What did you say?' said Wyatt.

'I said you're a yellow-bellied coward.'

'What would you know?' Wyatt hissed. 'If you had left well enough alone then none of this would be happenin'. I gave you the opportunity to walk away but you're just too blamed stubborn.'

142

'He must be payin' you good,' Ford observed. 'Is it your job to get rid of me?'

Wyatt nodded. 'At this point.'

'How long you been workin' for him?'

'Two years. It don't affect how I do my job, just ~~how~~ I do it concernin' him.'

'How much is he payin' you?' Ford asked.

'Five thousand,' Wyatt answered.

'What are you goin' to tell Bass? Once word gets back to him that I've been killed, he's goin' to have marshals crawlin' all over Seattle,' Ford pointed out.

'Not if I tell him the men you were after weren't here and you left,' said Wyatt in dismissal of Ford's logic. 'They'll just think you went missing on the ride back.'

'Thought of everythin', haven't you?'

Wyatt smirked with pride. 'Pretty much.'

'Before you go ahead and shoot me, can I ask you one more question?' Ford said calmly. Wyatt shrugged casually, all sign of his previous nervousness gone. 'Sure, why not.'

'Everythin' you told me before, about Peacock. Is it true or was it all lies?'

'What does it matter?'

'It matters to me. I'm the one that's about to die,' Ford said. 'You could at least tell me that much.'

Wyatt thought about the request then shrugged his shoulders. 'What the hell. Yeah, it was mostly true. Not that it matters 'cause you'll be dead anyhow.' The six-gun in Wyatt's fist came up to eye level and remained rock steady. Ford stared down the open end of the barrel silently. The brave facade fell away and he clasped his hands in front of himself and begged for Wyatt not to shoot him.

'Please . . . please don't shoot me,' he stammered. 'I don't want to die.' Ford sank to his knees, hands still clasped together, his eyes locked on Wyatt.

'Get up,' the dishonourable man snarled.

'Please, Archie, you don't have to do this,' Ford whimpered and fell to all fours.

'I said get the hell up, or I'll shoot you there,' Wyatt sneered. 'All of the stories I've ever heard about the great Josh Ford never included him cowerin' like a dog.'

Ford raised his head and looked up into the leering face of Wyatt. The deputy marshal exuded an arrogant confidence and sense of supremacy but he could never have foreseen what happened next. Ford scooped a handful of dirt from the floor and flung it at Wyatt's face.

Reflexively, Wyatt shut his eyes, but some of the dirt had found its target. Blinded, he staggered slightly and his finger tightened on the trigger.

His six-gun discharged and the bullet flew over Ford's shoulder. Wyatt brushed frantically at his eyes, trying to clear his vision. He fired again but the shot was even wilder and gouged splinters from the far wall.

Ford took advantage of the reprieve and dived forward to grab hold of the butt of the Peacemaker. He ripped it from its holster and as he brought it up, he thumbed back the hammer. Without aiming, he squeezed the trigger and the Colt thundered. The slug took Wyatt low down, about an inch above his belt buckle.

The man went up on his toes and leaned forward, the

punch of the bullet felt like a sledgehammer to his middle. Wyatt cried out with despair as he realized what had happened. The wounded man righted himself and fought to bring his gun into line for another shot at Ford. The gesture was futile as Ford's Peacemaker barked again and the bullet took him high in the chest. Wyatt dropped his gun and sank to the ground, two large wet stains on his front. He fell onto his back, gasping for air, his lungs increasingly useless as they steadily filled with blood. Ford climbed to his feet, then he moved over and knelt beside the dying man. A thin trickle of blood ran from the corner of his mouth. 'I . . . I was wrong . . . . about you,' he gasped out. 'Should . . . . should have been more careful . . . shot you when . . . when I had the chance.'

'Too late for that now,' Ford said coldly. Wyatt's low chuckle became a gurgle and he coughed violently to clear his throat. 'Where are they, Wyatt?' Ford asked him. 'Before you cross over, tell me where they are.' Wyatt went glassy eyed and Ford thought that he'd passed out. He grabbed the man's face and shook him roughly to bring him back.

'Come on, Wyatt, talk to me,' Ford urged. 'Where are they?'

'House . . . house on the . . . hill,' Wyatt forced out. 'Or the Gold Club.'

'Who runs this end when he's away?' Wyatt remained silent. Ford shook him. 'Who, damn it? Tell me.'

'Two . . . two men,' Wyatt said weakly. 'Morris and Walsh. Then there's the . . . the bookkeeper.'

'What bookkeeper?' Ford asked. Wyatt mumbled

something incoherent. 'Come on, you son of a bitch, don't you die on me now,' Ford cursed. 'What book-keeper?'

'Finch,' he whispered. 'Tobias Finch.'

'What does he do, Wyatt?' No answer. 'Wyatt?' But it was no use. Wyatt's eyes had glazed over and his ragged breathing had finally stopped. 'Damn it,' Ford said through clenched teeth. He reached across and tore the deputy marshal's badge from Wyatt's shirt and stuffed it in his own pocket. Instead of just two men, there were five to deal with. Things kept getting better and better. His challenge seemed like an overwhelmingly steep mountain, and Ferguson/Peacock was at the top, untouchable and out of reach. Ford was determined to climb that mountain and knew the only way to do that was start at the bottom.

CHAPTER 20

In all of his travels, Ford had never seen anything like the Gold Club. It was a three-storey brick construction with rows of windows on each floor.

A large hand-painted sign in gold lettering hung above a grand entrance. By the sight of the men entering and exiting the club, Ford knew that he was severely underdressed and would stand out like a sore thumb. Thank God he had a badge.

Ford climbed the steps to the twin glass doors where his progress was blocked by a man in a black top hat and tails.

'Can I help you, sir?' he asked Ford with a condescending look and tone.

His mind flashed back to the hotel in Helena. He sure as hell wasn't going to put up with that again.

Ford showed the man his badge.

The doorman gave him a blank stare and said, 'Yes, sir?'

Ford dropped his hand to his six-gun and stated angrily, 'Mister, if my badge ain't enough to get me

147

through them damn doors, then I got me a Peacemaker that says otherwise. Now, it's your choice what you do next.'

The doorman thought for a moment then stepped to one side. With a blank expression and a calm voice, he replied, 'Yes, sir,' then held the door open for the marshal.

Ford entered into a large foyer with plush carpets, polished timber wall panels and a giant staircase that led to the first floor. To the right stood a long, hardwood counter with a gleaming top. Another man dressed the same as the doorman, stood to attention behind the desk. To the left stood a tall, solidly built man who Ford guessed was stationed there in case of trouble.

Ford walked over to the counter and the clerk asked, 'May I help you, sir?'

'I'm lookin' for a feller named Peacock. Is he here?'

The man eyed him warily before he answered. 'Yes, sir. Mr Peacock is in the lounge.'

'Which is where?' Ford said.

The man pointed towards a doorway to his left. 'Through there, sir.'

As Ford approached the doorway, it opened and a middle-aged man exited with a woman draped on his arm. She was scantily clad in bright red underwear, matching corset and a smile. The man whispered something to her which solicited a bubbly laugh.

They crossed to the stairs and hurriedly climbed them. Ford watched until they disappeared then looked at the desk clerk.

'Sporting woman, sir,' he said in way of explanation.

The deputy marshal turned his back and headed for the door.

'Excuse me, sir,' the clerk called after him, signalling the security man. 'You can't go in there.'

The big guard moved to block Ford's path. This was starting to get tiresome. He sighed.

'Are you goin' to move?' Ford asked him.

'No, sir.'

Ford nodded. 'OK then.'

The Peacemaker came clear of leather in a blur of movement and crashed against the big man's head with a sickening crunch. He dropped to the floor and remained still, a trickle of blood ran from the cut in his scalp.

Ford turned to the clerk. 'I'm goin' to shoot the next person to get in my way and tries to stop me.'

'You can't do that, sir,' the man blustered. 'If you do not leave immediately, I shall have to inform law enforcement.'

'I am law enforcement,' Ford called back over his shoulder as he walked through the doorway.

The inside of the lounge was similar to the foyer, except there was more of it. As he cast his gaze about, he saw at least ten more ladies working a room of maybe forty men.

Leather chairs were scattered throughout the room. Wall lamps cast a muted light but the dark décor made it seem insufficient. Cigar smoke hung heavily in the air and the occasional soft clink of decanter on glass filtered through the voices. In addition to the working girls, a number of waiters with trays kept up a constant circulation of service to their guests. One of the waiters approached Ford. 'May I help you, sir?' he asked politely.

'Emerson Peacock?' Ford asked. Without hesitation, he said, 'Follow me, sir.'

Ford trailed the man between chairs and patrons until he drew up short of a group of three men gathered around a small table that held half-filled glasses.

'Here you are, sir,' the waiter gestured to the table. 'Mr Peacock is seated with those gentlemen there.'

'Thank you,' said Ford.

'Would you like a drink, sir?' Ford shook his head. 'I won't be here that long.'

'Very well,' the waiter said and left Ford standing there.

He became aware of everyone in the room, especially those who cast gazes in his direction. Ferguson, as he knew him, had his back to Ford, but the other two were faced in his general direction. One of them looked up and frowned. He was a middle-aged man with salt and pepper hair and a bushy moustache, waxed and curled at the ends. 'Is there something you want?' he asked abruptly, giving Ford a derisive look. Ford closed on the group and dug into his pocket to retrieve Wyatt's badge. He tossed it on the table where it landed with a rattle.'Damn it, Wyatt. . . .' Ferguson started and turned in his seat. The man's eyes bulged when they focused, not on Wyatt, but Josh Ford. He attempted to regain his composure but he was visibly shaken, face pale.

'Wyatt's dead,' Ford informed him. 'But before he died, he told me a mighty interestin' story. About you,

150

and Morris, and Walsh.' Ford kept an eye on the other two men and was rewarded with a faint reaction at the mention of their names.

'What do you want?' Ferguson croaked.

'Wyatt said you were untouchable. Well, I'm here to tell you you're not and I aim to prove it,' Ford warned him.

'Just how to you intend to do that?' Ferguson asked.

'You'll have to wait and see,' Ford said, then looked at the others before adding, 'all of you.'

'Don't mess with me, Ford,' Ferguson hissed. 'Like Wyatt said, you can't touch me. And know this, you may have escaped once before, but I warn you, if you mess with me, I will kill you myself.'

'Wow,' Ford's voice dripped with sarcasm. 'Threatening a federal peace officer. I'll just add that to the list of charges when I arrest you. By the way, where's your lap dog, Hayes? I thought he might have been with Gibson when I caught up with him. He's dead by the way.'

'Get out!' Ferguson shouted. 'Before I have you removed!'

Every head in the room turned in their direction and Ford smiled at them.

'Sorry about the outburst, gents, it seems Lord Ferguson has had some rather bad news.'

They all stared at him blankly.

'Sorry, I forgot,' Ford apologized. 'You know him as Emerson Peacock.'

Still there was silence. The deputy marshal turned back to Ferguson whose face had turned scarlet.

'Tell me somethin'. How does a lowly seaman who

deserts his ship get to be a Lord anyway?' Ford said.

Ferguson's eyes flickered.

Ford smiled coldly. 'Do you want to know what gave you away? I'll tell you. The cat. When you had me flogged, you called it kissin' the Captain's Daughter. That's how I knew. After a while, I pieced it together. And I bet you've got scars on your back, too.'

Another flicker of eyes.

'Yeah,' Ford said. 'I thought so.'

Without another word, Ford walked towards the door. As he reached it he turned and addressed the room once more. 'By the way. You might want to ask him how he came by most of his money. His illegal activities may surprise you.'

Then Ford was gone.

'What are we going to do about him?' Morris whispered harshly.

'Kill him, you fool,' Ferguson hissed back. 'What else?'

'You've tried that already and look how it turned out,' Morris pointed out.

'It will have to be soon,' Walsh stated. 'Or this will get too far out of hand. This was never meant to come back on us. You said it was too far away.'

'Don't worry, I'll take care of it. Besides, he can't touch us,' Ferguson assured them.

'You'd better hope so,' Walsh insisted. 'Or we'll all find ourselves at the end of a rope.'

'And you'd better watch your bloody tongue or you'll end up in the same hole in the ground as him,' Ferguson advised him.

CHAPTER 21

'You can't touch me.' The words rang in Ford's ears as he stood outside the club and tried to figure out his next move.

After considerable contemplation, he knew that Ferguson was right, and the thought irked him.

If he arrested the son of a bitch for everything he'd done, there was a still a good chance that he would walk free.

He thought about the lives that Ferguson had ruined. About Brady and old man Ellis and the others who'd died making these men rich. When he thought of the women who'd been used by the guards, he knew that Ferguson was responsible for that, too.

Ford looked down at the badge pinned to his chest. It weighed heavily on him at that moment and he knew what he had to do.

He removed the badge and placed it in his pocket. His next moves were better performed without it.

*

Ford waited and watched from the shadows. Light shone dimly through the windows of the two-storey house on the hill. It was surrounded on three sides by large trees while at the front it was clear, providing an unimpeded outlook across Seattle to the docks and beyond.

A fresh ocean scent was carried gently on the chill night breeze.

Ford was certain that there were four people, all men, on the premises. Two were outside, the others indoors. He guessed without a doubt that the two inside were Ferguson and Hayes.

He knew that his imminent actions were, in the eyes of the law, wrong. The knowledge did not deter him from his plans. He needed to proceed to gain justice for the innocents that Ferguson had imprisoned and killed.

High up in the starry sky, a cloud scudded across the moon. The landscape was enveloped briefly in darkness before the dull silvery glow returned after the cloud passed.

Ford reached down to his belt and drew the wickedly sharp knife that Yellow Bull had given him. He'd left his rifle in the saddle scabbard on the roan but still had his Peacemaker.

Veiled by the shadows, Ford approached the big house with frequent pauses. Both men walked the house's perimeter which would make Ford's job easy.

He waited until they crossed paths at the front of the house then slipped from a darkened patch of brush and moved quickly in behind the first man.

He clamped his hand over the man's mouth and thrust violently with the knife. The man stiffened as the knife slid off a rib and bit deep. Meeting no more resistance, it travelled up into the man's heart.

The first man was dead before Ford lowered his body to the ground. Ford melted back into the shadows to wait for the other man.

He didn't have to wait long before the silhouette of a man emerged cautiously around the corner of the house. His rifle was up and ready to use, his senses heightened and alert after his companion hadn't appeared on the other side.

Ford heard a harsh whisper escape the man's lips but he couldn't make out what was said. The man continued on until he stumbled across the corpse on the damp ground.

'What the hell?' Ford heard him gasp as he went to his knee beside the dead man.

Once more, Ford slunk from the shadows, a faceless figure with death in his hand.

The man must have sensed Ford's presence because he turned and began to bring up his rifle.

Ford crashed into him and knocked the wind from the man with a loud whoosh. With his right hand, he brought the butt of the knife handle down and dealt the man a savage blow to the top of his head.

The man ceased his struggle and went limp under Ford's weight. The deputy marshal rolled off the man and checked him for signs of life. He found none. The man's six-gun was removed from its holster and tucked into Ford's belt beside the knife.

Keeping low, Ford worked his way around to the front of the house. He eased his way up the steps and crossed to the main door. He paused and listened for any sign of someone on the other side.

When all remained silent, he reached out for the doorknob with his left hand, and with his right, drew his Peacemaker and thumbed back the hammer.

Ford twisted the knob and felt the door give as it swung free from the jamb. He moved it ajar sufficiently to admit his large frame, then closed it gently behind him.

The foyer was large and extravagantly furnished. The stairs that led to the second floor were wide and lined with a timber balustrade while a large chandelier hung from an ornate ceiling rose.

Ford looked about, unsure whether his quarry would be on the upper or ground floor. He spotted a light that shone out from under a closed door to his right.

That would be it.

He crossed to the door and paused briefly before opening it. Without hesitation, he entered the room, the Colt Peacemaker at waist level.

Both men in the room were startled by the sudden intrusion. Hayes dropped the glass of whiskey he held and his hand streaked for his gun.

'Don't!' Ford snapped, staying the hand. 'Just leave it be.'

Ferguson looked at Ford and said calmly, 'If you fire that weapon, Mr Ford, my men will be alerted and be in here in a flash.'

'Do you mean them two fellers that I killed on the way in here?'

Ferguson paled while Hayes remained stone-faced.

'What is it you want?' Ferguson asked.

'I think you know what I want, but in case you're a little slow on the uptake, I'll spell it out for you. I'm here to kill you. Call it payback for all you've done.'

A crack appeared in the Englishman's façade. 'You can't do that. You're the law, you can't just shoot people, you have to take them in for trial.'

Ford shrugged. 'True, but like you said earlier, you would likely get off. And if you haven't noticed, I ain't wearin' a badge.'

'I ain't just goin' to let you shoot me down like a dog, Ford,' Hayes snarled. 'Damned if I will.'

'And I'm unarmed,' Ferguson protested, hoping that it would be enough to save his life. 'That would be murder.'

Ford smiled coldly. 'Why should that worry me? It didn't worry you out in the Bitterroots.'

A thin bead of sweat appeared on the Englishman's forehead.

'I tell you what, I'll give you a chance,' Ford told the scared megalomaniac and reached down to the six-gun in his belt.

He tossed it across to Ferguson and the Englishman caught it in his fumbling grasp.

'Now you've got a gun,' Ford pointed out.

'No! Wait!' Ferguson screeched.

Ford ignored him and turned to Hayes. 'Anytime you're ready.'

'You have me at a disadvantage,' Hayes informed him, pointing to the drawn Peacemaker.

'Make do. It's all the advantage you're goin' to get.'

Hayes shook his head. 'Son of a bitch.'

The words had just left the outlaw's mouth and his shoulder dipped as his hand streaked for his gun.

Ford waited until Hayes had started his draw before he squeezed the trigger. His six-gun roared in the close confines of the room and the slug punched into Hayes' chest with a hollow thump.

Ford fired again and the bullet made an identical hole a finger's width from the other wound. Hayes was thrown back and as he went down, he knocked over a small table that held a kerosene lamp which broke and doused the carpeted floor with burning fuel.

Ford swivelled at the waist and brought the Peacemaker into line with Ferguson. The man had not moved.

'Wait!' he screamed shrilly when faced with his own mortality. 'I'm not going to shoot!'

'You should've,' Ford said flatly and squeezed the trigger.

Ford entered the governor's office to find Reynolds in a heated discussion with United States Marshal Bass Reeves. A week had passed since Ford had cleared up the issue in Seattle and he was not long off the train.

In his hand, Reynolds held a newspaper and waved it about madly. He looked up and spotted Ford.

'Did you do this?' he half shouted, and shoved the newspaper in front of Ford.

Ford read the headlines.

SEATTLE'S RICHEST MAN
SHOT DOWN IN OWN HOME
AND MANSION BURNED DOWN!

Ford looked at Bass then back at Reynolds.

'I did the job you wanted me to do.'

'So it was you!' Reynolds fumed. 'I'll have your badge for this.'

'Now hold on, Edmond,' Bass Reeves said in a stern voice. 'Ford did what he had to do to get the job done. I looked into this feller and I can tell you now, if this had made it to trial, he would never have been convicted.'

'So you condone this?'

'I'm sayin' that if it was me instead of Ford, I would have done the same thing. You seem to forget this man was responsible for the deaths of many people, includin' two of your own.'

'But. . . .' Reynolds started to protest further, his voice trailed away as he thought about Brady.

'Now if that's all, we'll be leavin',' Reeves said. Reynolds looked at Ford. 'Thank you for your services, Mr Ford.' Reynolds's voice was calm but clipped.

Once outside, Ford turned to Reeves. 'What did you do about the other three?'

'I've sent marshals to Seattle to clean up the mess,' Reeves told him. 'I'm sorry about Wyatt. I had no idea.'

Ford shrugged his shoulders uncomfortably and said, 'Thanks for your support in there.'

'Don't worry about it none. You did right, so don't let it get to you. Like I said, I would have done the same thing.'

Ford's face grew serious. 'If you think this'll make everythin' OK between us, think again.'

'Don't worry Josh, I wouldn't dream of it.'